MID-CONTINENT PUBLIC LIBRARY

3 0000 13301226 4

D0097403

WITHDRAWN
FROM THE RECORDS OF THE
MID-CONTINENT PUBLIC LIBRARY

Mid-Continent Public Library
15616 East US Highway 24
Independence, MO 64050

SPECIAL MESSAGE TO READERS

This book is published under the auspices of

THE ULVERSCROFT FOUNDATION

(registered charity No. 264873 UK)

Established in 1972 to provide funds for research, diagnosis and treatment of eye diseases. Examples of contributions made are: —

A Children's Assessment Unit at Moorfield's Hospital, London.

•

Twin operating theatres at the Western Ophthalmic Hospital, London.

•

A Chair of Ophthalmology at the Royal Australian College of Ophthalmologists.

•

The Ulverscroft Children's Eye Unit at the Great Ormond Street Hospital For Sick Children, London.

You can help further the work of the Foundation by making a donation or leaving a legacy. Every contribution, no matter how small, is received with gratitude. Please write for details to:

THE ULVERSCROFT FOUNDATION,
The Green, Bradgate Road, Anstey,
Leicester LE7 7FU, England.
Telephone: (0116) 236 4325

In Australia write to:
THE ULVERSCROFT FOUNDATION,
c/o The Royal Australian and New Zealand
College of Ophthalmologists,
94-98 Chalmers Street, Surry Hills,
N.S.W. 2010, Australia

RICHARD A. LUPOFF

THE UNIVERSAL HOLMES

Complete and Unabridged

LINFORD
Leicester

First published in Great Britain

First Linford Edition
published 2012

Copyright © 2007 by Richard A. Lupoff
All rights reserved

British Library CIP Data

Lupoff, Richard A., 1935 –
   The universal Holmes.- -
   (Linford mystery library)
   1. Holmes, Sherlock (Fictitious character)- -
   Fiction. 2. Detective and mystery stories,
   American. 3. Large type books.
   I. Title II. Series
   813.5′4–dc23

   ISBN 978–1–4448–1221–3

Published by
F. A. Thorpe (Publishing)
Anstey, Leicestershire

Set by Words & Graphics Ltd.
Anstey, Leicestershire
Printed and bound in Great Britain by
T. J. International Ltd., Padstow, Cornwall

This book is printed on acid-free paper

One

The Adventure of
The Older Sister

I was womanning the counter, waiting upon customers, accepting payments and wrapping baked goods, when the postman's bell was heard in the courtyard. I refuse to refer to myself a 'manning' anything. Such usage demeans the female gender and implies that I am in some manner inferior to and subservient to the male.

Mr. Tolliver leaned his bicycle against the postern and, after taking a moment to sort through his sack of mail, came forward and handed me a handful of missives. He smiled through his gray moustache. 'Mum all right, Miss Holmes?'

'She would rather work,' I replied, 'but the doctor insists that she rest during these final weeks. Once the new arrival is here, he says, she will have work enough to do.'

'Aye. And Dad, what has he to say?'

'He is in league with Doctor Millward.

As am I. Mother insists on cooking for us all, but at least she has consented to allow the rest of us to run the shop.'

I handed Mr. Tolliver a complimentary crumpet and he retrieved his bicycle and pedaled away.

The shop was busy this day. It was all that young Sherlock could do keeping up with mixing batters, keeping the ovens in order, and placing fresh goods on display. Dad alternated caring for Mum and napping so he would have his strength to tend to the heavy baking duties overnight. And of course Mycroft sat in the nook that passed for an office, working as he ever did over the bakery's books and studying formulas for new products.

Mycroft also handled our correspondence, such as it was, ordering supplies and paying bills. Ours was a reasonably successful family business, but a most demanding one in this busy section of London. Competition was keen, as well.

By the time the shop was closed for the day darkness had fallen over London and gas lamps were casting soft shadows outside our dwelling. Gas had also been installed indoors despite the grumbles of older residents who insisted that the new lighting was unnatural and unpleasant compared to the traditional oil lamps.

Father had risen from a nap. Mum had made a rich soup of orange pumpkin and had roasted us a piece of beef with potatoes and greens. There were, of course, baked goods from our own shop. Mycroft was as usual prompt to reach his place at the family table. It seems that Mycroft spends his entire life in a stationary posture, save for his rare and unexplained 'expeditions.' At irregular intervals he will rise ponderously, don headpiece, take walking stick in hand, and disappear for an hour or a day.

On one occasion that I recall he was gone for an entire year without a trace. My parents had given him up for lost when he strode into the shop, greeted a number of our regular customers familiarly, and returned to his accustomed place without a word of explanation. My elder brother is as portly as my younger is scrawny; could they but exchange a few stone of avoirdupois I believe they would both be the better off.

But this night, and I refer to the night upon which Mother had, despite her gravid condition, prepared for us a hearty and delicious repast. It fell to me to summon Sherlock who had retreated to his room to practice his fiddle-playing.

I do not know which is more distressing, the sounds of scraping and screeching that he calls music or the unpleasant odors of the chemical experiments, which he conducts from time to time. Why my parents had gifted me with this bothersome stringbean of a younger brother is beyond human comprehension. I hoped only that the next addition to the Holmes household would be a pleasanter companion. The Fates willing, a girl!

Of course, this pregnancy is a late and unanticipated one. Still, Mother gives every evidence of pleasure at the prospect of having another Holmes about the house. Father worries about expenses. Mycroft appears oblivious.

As for the execrable Sherlock, I suppose that he is accustomed to the privileges associated with being the youngest member of the household. When mention is made of the fact that he will lose this distinction his expression resembles that of a person who has bitten into a fruit, thinking it an orange, only to discover that it is a lemon.

To be honest I will confess that my little brother is not entirely brainless. On one occasion which I recall, he asked me to assist him in his so-called laboratory. He explained that he was developing a technique to transmit energy by means of sound waves. He had arranged an experiment in which he mounted a metallic object in a brace, surrounded by sound-absorbing batting. He stood nearby, scraping hideous sounds from his fiddle. He played notes higher and higher in pitch until, to my astonishment, the metal object began to vibrate violently.

'Now, sister, I want you to stand on the other side of the apparatus and match that note on your flute.'

I complied, with similar results.

'And now,' Sherlock proclaimed, 'for the peas of resistance. We shall stand on either side of the apparatus, and upon my signal, both sound the keynote.'

I did not correct his solecism but merely shook my head in exasperated compliance.

Sherlock placed his fiddle beneath his chin, laid bow across strings, and favored me with a nod and a wink. The grotesquery of that bony visage thus distorted far exceeds my mean verbal powers. Indeed, the awfulness of it must be imagined rather than described.

We both sounded the crucial note, he upon his fiddle and I upon my flute. Within seconds the metal object began to vibrate violently, then to glow with red heat, and finally to liquefy and fall in a silvery rain upon the floor.

At this moment, Mother entered the room. 'Elisabeth, Sherlock, dears, has either of you seen my precious silver spoon from Her Majesty's Silver Jubilee?'

Alas, there it lay, a formless puddle of molten metal upon the floor of Sherlock's laboratory.

* * *

The meal proceeded pleasantly enough, each family member in turn describing his or her day as is our longstanding custom. Talk had turned to affairs of the world as they filtered into our household through the conversation of our customers when Mycroft announced that he had found a missive addressed to our parents in the day's arrivals.

Mycroft is by far the most brilliant man I have ever encountered. I cannot imagine him spending his life in our family bakery, but for the time being he performs invaluable service. He can also be the most exasperating of men, surpassing even the annoying Sherlock. Wiping his chin free of a drop of grease he muttered and patted himself here and there, searching for whatever it was that he meant to give me.

At last he found it. He drew it from an inner pocket and handed it to Father.

It was an envelope carefully addressed to *Mr and Mrs. Reginald Beasley Holmes, in care of Holmes Family Bakery, Old Romilly Street, London, England.* The stamps were of an unfamiliar hue and design, denominated in something called 'cents.' A return address in the City of New York in the United States of America provided the solution to the mystery of the odd stamps.

There followed an act that could have been performed as a comic turn at a Cheapside music hall. Father patted himself upon the chest, blinking all the time. 'I cannot find my spectacles,' he announced at last, handing the envelope to Mother.

Mother shook her head. 'I must tend to my kitchen duties. Perhaps one of the children will read this letter to us all.'

Somehow the duty fell to my lot. Somehow, it seems, in this household it always does.

I opened the envelope. It seemed to be unusually stiff and of a finer grade of paper than most ordinary correspondence is. From the envelope I extracted a card. In embossed lettering it read as follows:

Mr. and Mrs. Jorgen Sigerson
Request the pleasure of your company
At the wedding of their daughter,
Miss Inga Elisabeth Sigerson
To Mr. Jonathan Van Hopkins

In the City of New York
On the first Sunday of June, 1875

I had read the card aloud. Upon hearing it Mother clapped her hands. 'My dear brother's child is to be married! It seems but yesterday that she was an infant.'

'I knew it,' I could not keep myself from exclaiming. 'I knew that a wonderful event was about to befall my Cousin Inga.'

'A joyous occasion indeed, but of course we shall send our regrets,' Father stated. 'The first of June is mere weeks ahead. There is no way that Mum could possibly undertake an ocean voyage, nor would I under the circumstances even consider traveling to America while she remained at home to face the arrival of our new child.'

Mother reached for the envelope and I extended it toward her. As I did so a slip of paper fell from it, barely missing the vegetable bowl and landing in front of the bony Sherlock. He snatched it up and refused to surrender it until Father commanded him to do so. Even so, I had to tug at the slip before he would release it.

The note was written in the familiar hand of my cousin. *Dearest Elisabeth, I* read silently, *My Jonathan is the most wonderful man. He is a skilled printer and editor and we plan to move to the West once married. Please, please, Cousin dearest, do find a way to come to my wedding. I shall be heartbroken if you do not. I want you there as my Maiden of Honor.* The note was signed, in my cousin's customary manner, with a cartoon drawing of the two of us.

Although we have never met, I believe that we have had a psychic link throughout our lives. My mother and her father were twins. Mother remained here in England while her brother emigrated to the United States, where he married an American woman. Even so, we two cousins were born on the same day, and as far we have been able to determine, at the same moment. My cousin was named Inga Elisabeth and I was named Elisabeth Inga.

The invitation to my dear cousin's joyous nuptials was confirmation of a knowledge that I had carried for weeks.

Gathering my courage I announced that, in view of my parents' inability to do so, I would represent the English branch of the family at Inga's wedding.

Father shook his head. 'Out of the question, Elisabeth. We shall obtain a suitable gift for your cousin and dispatch it by transatlantic transport. You will not travel to America, certainly not alone.'

Mother fingered the strings that held her apron in place, tying and untying them in distress. 'Inga is my brother's only child, Reginald, Elisabeth's only cousin. It would be sad if she could not be present on this occasion.'

'No,' Father insisted, 'a young woman traveling alone under these conditions would be most improper.'

'Perhaps her brother could go with her, then. Mycroft is a responsible young man. Surely he would be a suitable chaperone for Elisabeth, and I have no doubt that my brother and sister-in-law would welcome him into their home.'

I will confess that even in this moment I found it amusing to think of Mycroft boarding a ship and traveling to America. Mycroft, whose daily movements seldom exceed the distance from bedroom to office, from office to dinner table, from dinner table to parlor, and from parlor to bedroom.

With a single word Mycroft negatived our Mum's suggestion, nor was any further discussion useful.

Following dinner and coffee we retired to the parlor for our customary Family Hour. Some evenings Mother will read aloud from a popular work of fiction. Others, I play familiar airs on my flute, on occasion accompanied by Sherlock's execrable fiddle-scratching. Rarely, Mycroft deigns to entertain us with a recitation. He has committed to memory the complete *Dialogues* of Plato, Plutarch's *Lives of Famous Men,* the scientific works of the great Mr. Charles Darwin. And the Reverend Dodgson's *Adventures of Alice in Wonderland,* a favorite of my own from earliest childhood.

But this evening there was but a single

topic of conversation. It was the wedding of my cousin.

Mother and Father having ruled out their own presence at the nuptials, Father having forbad me to travel alone, and Mycroft having refused to contemplate the journey, there remained but one possible solution to the puzzle. I swallowed my pride and proposed that Sherlock might accompany me.

I half hoped that he would reject the idea. To be honest, I more than half hoped as much. But my dear younger sibling took this occasion to torment me by giving his assent. Of course he did so with a demonstration of reluctance bordering upon martyrdom.

Mother seemed ready to give her blessing to this plan when Father raised the question of money. Fare for two persons traveling from England to America and back would come to a substantial amount. It might be possible to run the bake shop without Sherlock and myself for a time. Father could call upon friends and even the great Mycroft might move his ponderous self from desk to counter.

But there was simply not sufficient funds in the till to provide passage for Sherlock and myself.

Father rose from his chair. He assured himself that Mother was all right, then announced that he would proceed to his duties in the shop. 'And we will send a suitable gift, perhaps a gravy boat or salver, to the happy bride.'

'Not yet.' Mycroft's words, spoken in the same rich voice that he used for his learned recitations, brought Father to a halt.

'Not yet?' Father echoed.

'Sir,' Mycroft replied, 'do not be so quick, Father, to give up on our family's being represented at the wedding. Remember that Inga is my cousin as well, and I would wish to see my sister and her cousin together on the happy day.'

Father looked puzzled. He reached for his spectacles, unfolded their arms and placed them on his face to get a better look at his elder son. 'I trust you do not plan to rob a bank, Mycroft, in behalf of Elisabeth and Sherlock.' Father seldom makes jokes but I believe he thought he

16

had just done so.

'Never mind what I plan, Father. Please trust me. I make no promise, but I venture that Elisabeth and Sherlock will be at Inga's wedding.' He reached into his vest pocket and extracted a turnip. After consulting it he shook his head. 'Too late this evening,' he said. 'Give me twenty-four hours, Father. I ask no more.'

The next morning found our bake shop fully stocked as usual, the product of Father's industry. I took my place at the counter; Sherlock, his in the area reserved for handling goods; and Mycroft, at his desk, tending to his administrative duties. Nothing further was spoken of last night's family conference.

At noontime Mycroft rose, took hat and walking stick, and strode from the shop. He disappeared into the pedestrian traffic of Old Romilly Street. He did not appear again until the family had gathered at the dinner table.

Mother had roasted a chicken and small potatoes, hot and cold greens, and of course dinner rolls and butter. She took her place at the head of the table;

Father, at the foot; Sherlock and I, facing each other across the cloth and dishes. Father had just taken carving implements in hand and reached for the brown-crusted bird when Mycroft entered the room. He rubbed his hands together, smiled at each family member in turn, and took his place.

He spoke at length during the meal, but his sole topic was the excellence of Mother's cooking and Father's baking. 'We are not the possessors of financial wealth,' he stated, 'but we are a fortunate family to have a comfortable home, a successful business, one another's company, and the finest cuisine, in my humble judgment, in all the realm.'

He may have exaggerated but none at the table chose to dispute him. Not even Sherlock.

Following our meal the family assembled in the parlor, at which time Mycroft actually stood rather than sitting, and made his announcement.

'All is arranged,' he said. 'I met this afternoon with certain persons, and it is done.'

'You have tickets for us?' Sherlock asked. His voice is less discordant and irritating than his playing upon the fiddle, but not much so.

'Tickets? No, Sherlock. You will not need tickets.'

'Oh, a riddle, is it, Mycroft?' Sherlock ground his teeth audibly.

'If you wish, stripling. Or if you would rather, I will simply explain matters in words comprehensible even to so mean an intellect as yours.'

'Please,' I put in. 'Mycroft, do not lower yourself to the child's level.' Even though, I thought, the scrawny beanpole is already the tallest member of our household. 'Just tell us what you have done.'

'Very well.' Mycroft did lower himself now into his chair. Mother had served coffee and sweet pastries from the shop and Mycroft placed an apricot pastry upon his tongue. He chewed and swallowed with evident pleasure. 'As you may know,' he said, 'the *Great Eastern* departs from London on the fifteenth of May. She crosses the Atlantic in eleven

19

days, arriving in New York on the twenty-sixth. I believe that will provide ample time for you and Cousin Inga to work with Aunt Tanner upon the trousseau.'

'Yes, yes, Mycroft. But how can Sherlock,' I shuddered at the thought, 'and I travel on the *Great Eastern* when we have no tickets and no money with which to buy them?'

'Dinner music and entertainment is provided aboard the *Great Eastern* by the orchestra of Mr. Clement Ziegfried. You are an accomplished pianist and flautist, dear sister, while young Sherlock,' and Mycroft shuddered visibly, 'does on occasion manage to scrape a recognizable melody from his instrument. I have arranged for you both to become members of Mr. Ziegfried's musical aggregation. Passage and meals will be provided, and a modest stipend will be paid.'

There was a silence in the room, broken at last by Mycroft himself, 'There is one minor consideration, however.'

Sherlock grinned.

I waited.

'A small cabin will be made available for your use, but you will have to share it. In the interest of propriety you will be expected to travel as brothers.'

I moaned.

Sherlock laughed.

'Why not as sisters, then?' I asked.

Mycroft grinned. He has a most adorable, winning grin, has my elder brother. 'A splendid thought, Elisabeth. Most amusing.' He paused to sip at his coffee. 'Alas, it is already arranged that the Holmes Brothers, Ellery and Sherlock, are to perform with the Ziegfried orchestra.'

Eleven days, I thought. The voyage would take eleven days. That would mean eleven days of passing for a male and eleven nights of sharing a stuffy ship's cabin with my brother Sherlock. I shuddered.

And so it was settled. I persuaded my good friend Clarissa Macdougald who lives two houses from us and with whom I attended school for many years, to take my place in the shop. Her brother would substitute for Sherlock. Father approved the arrangement. I take pride in my skill with needle and scissors, learned from Mother. The two of us altered male clothing to fit my needs and to conceal my gender.

Sherlock and I arose long before dawn on the fifteenth of May and made our way by rail from London to Southampton. Once in that southerly city it would have been impossible not to find our destination.

The *Great Eastern* was famed as the greatest nautical achievement since Noah's Ark. It was known, as well, to carry a curse. Two workmen had died in the great iron ship's launching some seventeen years ago. Her designer, the genius Isambard Kingdom Brunel, had perished at an early age, doubtless due at least in part to the stress of his enterprise. The ship's bottom had been ripped by a hitherto unknown underwater mountain on one of her early voyages, and only Brunel's brilliant design of a double hull had saved her from sinking. She had been designed to carry as many as 4,000 passengers but had never been a commercial success.

Even so, and despite my having seen many images of the nautical behemoth, my first sight of her took my breath.

Sherlock and I were clothed in similar garments. We wore tweed suiting, knicker-bocker trousers, plain cravats, caps upon our heads and brogans upon our feet. I found the male garb uncomfortable and impractical. I yearned for a proper frock and flowered spring hat, even an outfit of blouse and jumper. But if this unpleasant costume was the price of my being accepted as Ellery rather than Elisabeth, it was a price I was willing to pay.

While Sherlock was in fact my junior by some five years, whiskers were already beginning to make themselves visible upon his upper lip, while my own countenance, of course, was unblemished by such excrescences. Thus, it had been decided that Sherlock Holmes would pass as the older of the musical siblings while Ellery Holmes would be the younger. A further insult to me, I felt.

Sherlock and I each carried a gripsack containing toiletries and changes of costume, and a separate case containing our respective musical instruments. We had been warned that the ship's orchestra were expected to appear in proper dinner costumes, and with Mother's deft management and my own long hours of sewing, Sherlock and I had so furnished ourselves. We made, I am sure, a picturesque couple.

We were met at the head of the *Great Eastern's* gangplank by a ship's officer, who directed us to our quarters. There we met Mr. Clement Ziegfried, our maestro. He was a harried-looking person. He wore his dark hair quite long, as was, I believe, not uncommon among members of the musical fraternity, and a luxuriously drooping moustache that seemed too heavy for his small face and thin neck.

He smiled and shook Sherlock's hand and my own. He said, 'Holmes major and minor, yes, welcome. I see you have brought your instruments with you. Good! You are of course unfamiliar with my orchestra's repertoire.' He paused and consulted a turnip that he pulled from a brocade weskit. 'We have rehearsal in twenty-two and one-third minutes in the grand salon. Place your belongings in your cabin and present yourselves promptly, if you please!' He spoke with a peculiar accent, obviously Continental.

He turned on his heel and strode away.

He was a very strange little man.

Because the *Great Eastern* was so huge — longer than two football pitches laid end to end — and had space for so many passengers, room was not at a premium. I had expected to have to live in cramped quarters with dozens of smelly males. Instead, Sherlock and I were housed in a comfortable cabin of our own. Each of us would of course have a bunk of her or his own. And having lived for twenty-two years as Mycroft's younger sister and for seventeen as Sherlock's older, I was not shy about enduring the mundane presence of a male.

We deposited our gripsacks in our cabin, found a crewman on deck and were directed to the grand salon. This was a spacious chamber, clearly a living souvenir of the *Great Eastern's* glory days. The walls were decorated with friezes of classical scenes. Satyrs and caryatids stood in classical poses, supporting the high, domed ceiling of the salon. That ceiling was of stained glass, a magnificent design that would have done proud any architectural showplace in the land.

The musicians assembled upon a small dais. Sherlock and I were apparently the last to join them. Maestro Ziegfried stood before us, half hidden by a black music stand, turnip in hand. The watch buzzed audibly. Maestro silenced it by pressing a lever and returned it to his weskit pocket. He surveyed the assembled musicians and nodded his satisfaction.

'Gentlemans,' he announced, 'we have three new musicians with us for this journey. I will introduce them to you.' He lifted a baton and tapped it on his music stand.

'Mr. Holmes major.'

Sherlock bowed slightly, holding his fiddle at the height of his shoulder.

'Mr. Holmes minor.'

I emulated my brother, showing my flute to my fellow musicians.

'Mr. Albert Saxe.'

A portly musician standing in the second row bowed slightly, holding a glittering trumpet in the air. He wore a moustache and beard. How he could maneuver his trumpet through that hirsute decoration was a puzzle to me.

Speaking in his oddly accented manner Maestro Ziegfried announced that each of us would find sheet music before us. 'You will take six minutes and twenty-three seconds to acquaint yourselves with the notes. Then we rehearse.'

What an odd man he was! Still, one followed his directions. My parents had replied to my Cousin Inga's wedding invitation, expressing their regrets and enclosing a token wedding gift for the bride and groom. I had dispatched a personal note as well, telling Inga that Sherlock and I would arrive on the *Great Eastern* and anticipated the occasion of her nuptials with the greatest joy.

And of course, I would be happy, thrilled, honored, and delighted to participate as maiden of honor. I was certain, also, that her fiancé, Mr. Van Hopkins, would prove a splendid individual whom I would be pleased to accept as a cousin-in-law, were there such a position in the rules of family relationships.

With a blast of her whistle the *Great Eastern* pulled away from her dock and moved into the channel toward Portsmouth, rounded land and headed in a westerly direction. By the time we passed Penzance the orchestra was warmed up. Maestro Ziegfried was a stern leader. There was no concertmaster; he coached and prodded the musicians himself, shaking his head with joy or anger or passion at each passage until his long hair flew around his head like the wings of an angry black bird.

When rehearsal ended, Maestro laid his baton upon his music stand and pulled his turnip from his pocket. He pressed a lever and the watch's engraved metal cover sprang open. He studied the watch's face, then nodded and announced, 'Gentlemans, you will assemble here ready to perform in one hour, fifty-six minutes and eleven seconds.'

He jammed his watch in his pocket,

turned on his heel, and took his departure.

Although I had stood for Mother to prepare my suit of dinner clothes I had never worn this strange black-and-white costume for any extended period of time, nor attempted to perform even the meanest of tasks in it. How strange and uncomfortable it was, with its stiff wing collar, miniature black cravat, satin lapels and itchy woolen trousers. What in the world is the matter with the male gender that they choose to get themselves up in such impractical outfits!

The *Great Eastern's* passengers had already begun filtering into the grand salon when the orchestra assembled, strictly on time per our Maestro's eccentric directions. I found myself seated beside another flautist, a gentleman with round, rose-colored cheeks and white hair. I could not tell whether he was prematurely white-haired, amazingly well-preserved, or perhaps was simply the possessor of Scandinavian blood and blond hair so pale as to appear blond.

My Brother Sherlock, I saw, was immersed in a section of violins, violas, and violoncellos. *Good,* I thought, *there are enough of them to drown him out. Or maybe he will have the sense to hold his bow a fraction off the strings and avoid making any noise at all!*

Waiters were serving beverages and food to the passengers. The *Great Eastern* is so huge that a virtual barnyard of cattle and poultry is kept on her deck, providing fresh provisions for all during her voyages.

Maestro had planned a program that mixed recent works by the great composers of Europe with popular tunes suitable for performance in the music halls of England and America. For some selections only parts of the orchestra were required to perform. Maestro called upon the string section for a new quartet by the young Bohemian musical folklorist Dvorak. This was followed by a full orchestral rendering of an American tune by Luke Schoolcraft. Clearly influenced by what I believe is called 'darkie music,' this jolly piece, titled *Oh! Dat Watermelon!* was indeed a rouser.

Between numbers when I was not busy shuffling the sheets upon my music stand,

I scanned the tables of well-dressed diners. For all that the *Great Eastern* had proved a commercial failure as a passenger liner, she had been turned to a number of other uses with far greater success. That she had been refitted for her original purpose was a melancholy matter. Word was that she was to be sold and turned into some sort of commercial showboat, a floating advertisement hoarding, and moored in a resort town, perhaps Brighton or Torquay. This, the greatest ship in the world, which had been visited by Her Majesty herself, and by His Highness the Prince of Wales, on one or more occasions!

Still Captain Halpin and his officers maintained the appearance of grand sea sailors. Their uniforms were elaborate, as neatly tailored and sharply pressed as those of any naval officer, their buttons sparkling, their decorations looking like the awards granted to the victors of great marine engagements. The captain himself was a portly man, bearded and mustachioed in the manner made popular by the Prince of Wales. He was seen from time to time striding the *Great Eastern's* deck in company of his wife and three lovely daughters and their great dog Harold. How I envied those three girls their freedom to be themselves and not play-act at being boys!

The other diners in the salon were an assortment of well-dressed and groomed ladies and gentlemen. A few of them, I surmised, might be emigrants intending to make new lives for themselves in the Western Hemisphere. Canada and Newfoundland sounded attractive to me, especially the former. The United States with its red Indians, its many thousands of black former slaves, and its Irish gangs must be a dangerous and exciting nation. Soon enough I should find out for myself!

One man I noticed carrying on a particularly animated conversation. He chopped the air with hands in time to the music and jerked his head up and down in agreement with himself at every moment. He was apparently without companion, but was seated at a table with several couples who gave every appearance of discomfort with his expostulations. When he paused for breath he drew back his lips to reveal teeth that reflected the salon's gaslights, causing me to wonder if he had not had them drilled by the new electrical apparatus of Mr. George Green, and filled with a metal amalgam.

My attention was drawn back by the tapping of Maestro's baton upon his music stand. We were to perform a suite of flute duets by Wolfgang Mozart. The rosy-cheeked flautist at my side smiled encouragingly and we set out upon a sea of the loveliest music ever composed.

It pleases me to state that we started and ended together, the performance was not a disaster, and most of our auditors actually lowered their implements and hushed their conversations while we played. Maestro Ziegfried smiled and gestured to us to rise and take a bow at the conclusion of the suite, and the room applauded most generously. My fellow flautist shook my hand and gave me his name, Jenkins. He had, of course, already learned mine.

That night I sat up in my bunk composing a letter to Mother and Father.

I would post it when the *Great Eastern* reached New York. I was bursting with happiness. I was in the world at large. I had performed musically to acclaim. Even the presence in the other bunk of the annoying Sherlock could not dampen my cheery spirits.

As the voyage proceeded our days on shipboard were not unpleasant. Our meals were excellent in quality and generous in portion. When not rehearsing or performing, we musicians were free to roam the *Great Eastern's* extensive decks, to borrow volumes from her library, even to explore her gigantic engine rooms. These were extensive. She carried volumes of coal with which to fire the huge boilers that powered her twin paddle wheels and her screw propeller. The ship even bore tall masts, but her sails were seldom unfurled.

From time to time I would encounter my friend Mr. Jenkins. We even shared a glass of wine on occasion, discussing the great ship, Maestro Ziegfried, and various members of the orchestra. Mr. Jenkins seemed to have tidbits of gossip, most of it not unpleasant, about each of our fellow musicians, with the exception of the trumpeter, Mr. Saxe. When I asked if Mr. Jenkins knew anything of this gentleman he quickly changed the subject.

Our musical repertoire was varied, with each evening's performance including both orchestral and solo performances. Maestro Ziegfried proved an expert pianist, including compositions by Joseph Haydn, Frederic Chopin, and several of the Bachs, most notably my favorite, the underrated Carl Philipp Emanuel.

During Maestro's solo performances I was able to observe the audience. Time and again my attention was drawn to the man with the metallic teeth.

His behavior changed but little each evening. He would arrive at the appointed hour and take his place, the sole unaccompanied male sharing a table with three couples. At the beginning of the meal his mien was respectable, but he inevitably consumed copious alcoholic beverages. As he did so he became increasingly animated and, apparently, belligerent. On an evening near the end of our voyage, two days before we were due to make landfall at New York, his six companions rose in a body and departed from the table, leaving him to fume amidst empty bottles and soiled napkins.

Early the next afternoon Sherlock and I strolled upon the *Great Eastern's* deck. The starboard side was reserved for the ship's sea-going cattle ranch, as I had come to think of it. The port side was the promenade deck, so lengthy and broad that it had come to be known as Oxford Street.

Sherlock was speculating upon the availability of scientific instruments in the savage streets of New York. I listened patiently, or half-listened, pretending a greater interest in his monologue that in truth I felt. The *Great Eastern* must have been breasting a warm Atlantic current, perhaps the fabled Gulf Stream, for the air was warm and so moist that it seemed almost to hold a heavy mist. Figures appeared and disappeared as they approached or distanced themselves in what I finally came to think of as a displaced London fog.

A well-dressed couple approached us.

The gentleman bowed politely. 'Mr. Holmes and Mr. Holmes, is it not?'

My brother and I conceded that we were indeed the Holmeses.

'You are not really named Major and Minor, however?' Apparently these people were Americans, returning to their homeland. Had they been British they would have been familiar with the customary identification of elder and younger brothers.

'My name is Sherlock Holmes,' my beanpolish sibling explained. 'My little brother is Ellery.'

'Boatwright. Bertram and Bonnie Boatwright, of Back Bay, Boston,' the gentleman said.

There followed much tipping of hats and shaking of hands. I had to remind myself that I was one of three males in the presence of but one female. I would have liked to identify myself by my gender; I could imagine how Bonnie Boatwright must yearn for the companionship of a fellow woman, but I determined to maintain my disguise.

The Boatwrights invited Sherlock and

myself to join them in their stroll along 'Oxford Street.' Both of these Bostonians were kind enough to compliment me at length upon my rendering of the Mozart flute duets with Mr. Jenkins. No mention was made of Sherlock's violin performances. It was well, I thought, that Maestro had not singled my brother out for any solo.

The prow of our great ship split the waters gracefully. A thin spray, on occasion, rose above the ship's railing, reminding one and all that we were not in truth at home, but many hundreds of miles from the nearest land.

At length our conversation, which had consisted for the most part of what is sometimes known as 'small talk,' turned to the Boatwrights' dinner companion.

'It is a good thing that we are Americans,' Mr. Boatwright announced. 'That fellow — what is his name, darling?'

'Beaufort. John Gaunt Beaufort, or so he fancies himself.'

'Thank you, my dear. Beaufort. Yes. As I was saying, it is a good thing that we are

Americans, and your English politics with your dukes and princes and suchlike don't mean much to us.'

'And why is that?' piped Sherlock in his irritating voice.

'Why, young fellow, this Beaufort pipsqueak seems to think he's the King of England.'

There was a shocked silence.

Then Sherlock and I exclaimed simultaneously, 'What?'

'Yes, that's what he says.'

Mrs. Boatwright nodded agreement with her husband. 'Yes, he says that he is the rightful King of England.'

'Surely he means that as a jest,' I put in.

'I think not. Have you seen his conduct? He became so agitated that he knocked over a bottle of wine and ruined my poor darling's frock.'

'He is serious, then?'

'Very.'

'Upon what does he base his claim?'

'He says that he is the legitimate heir of the Plantagenets. That each monarch since Henry the Seventh has been an usurper and a fraud. That upon the death of Richard the Third the crown should rightfully have passed to Margaret Pole, eighth Countess of Salisbury. That her beheading in 1541 was an unforgivable crime and that only the recognition of this fellow, this — what was his name again, darling?'

'John Gaunt Beaufort,' Bonnie Boatwright dutifully supplied.

'Yes, this Beaufort fellow claims that the crown is rightfully his and that once he is recognized as rightful monarch of Great Britain and her Empire, he will take the name Richard the Fourth.' He shook his head in disbelief. 'Kept muttering about houses. Do you think he's a real estate developer?'

Bonnie Boatwright said, 'No, dear.'

Bertram Boatwright ignored her. 'Don't know why a real estate developer would complain about kings, eh, Holmeses?'

I felt compelled at this point to give the poor overlooked Mrs. Boatwright her due respect. Calling upon the authority of my *faux* manhood I interrupted. 'Mrs. Boatwright, what was your point regarding real estate?'

Her gratitude at even this small recognition of her worth was manifest. She said, 'Beaufort's reference to houses was directed at the dynasties of the British monarchy. At least, such was my education, even in Boston. He mutters about the Angevins, the Lancasters, and the Yorks. But he is most opposed to those who came later. To the Tudors, the Stuarts, and the Hanovers.'

Bertram Boatwright said, 'Quite right, my dear, quite right.' Then he shook his head. 'My manners, my manners,' he exclaimed, patting himself on the chest. From an inner pocket he drew an elaborate cigar case of yellow metal and green stone — I guessed, gold and jade — and opened it. 'Will you have a cheroot, Mr. Holmes?'

He extended the cigar case to Sherlock and to me. We each extracted a cigar from it.

'The finest Havana,' Bertram Boatwright announced. He drew a packet of lucifers from another pocket and struck one to light.

Sherlock bit the tip from his cheroot,

bent toward the flaring Lucifer that Mr. Boatwright held for him, and drew a flame into the cheroot.

This, I thought, will be the supreme test of my masquerade. I imitated my brother and managed to get the cigar going. I had expected to collapse upon the deck in a coughing fit, but instead I found the flavor of the smoke not unpleasant.

We soon parted from the Boatwrights and returned to our cabin. Sherlock sat upon his bunk, making arcane computations in a note book while I penned another missive to our parents in London.

I made it my business to arrive early that evening at the grand salon. Our voyage was drawing to a close. We expected to make land on the second day following, and a peculiar air had descended upon the ship. It was an amalgam of melancholy and excitement; the former, I suppose, deriving from the imminent dissolution of the little aquatic community that had formed on our ship; the latter, as women and men thought of the homes that awaited them or of the adventures they might experience in this exotic and undeveloped nation.

Mr. Beaufort made his entrance as usual. I thought that the night before he had drunk almost to the point of unconsciousness, and I rather expected him either to miss tonight's meal altogether, or to arrive shaken and contrite. No such symptoms, however, were visible.

The Boatwrights of Boston and the other couples who shared their table arrived in turn. They exchanged greetings with one another and even ventured a polite nod to the self-styled monarch who favored them with his company.

Maestro's selections of music for the evening were subdued for the most part, although the performance climaxed with a chamber arrangement of Peter Illich Tchaikovsky's *Pathétique* symphony — not the lugubrious piece that its title implied, but in fact a rousing composition.

Mr. Beaufort — I still thought of him as 'the man with the metal teeth' — managed to avoid any outbursts, and retired even before coffee and brandy had been served.

The next day was to be our last full day at sea. The *Great Eastern* had performed admirably and I was saddened to think that this would, in all likelihood, be her last oceanic crossing save one. That, of course, would be her return journey to England. I stayed up late composing another missive to my parents, then lay in my bunk, imagining the wedding to which I was journeying.

If I was in truth to serve as my cousin's Maiden of Honor I would of course need a suitable costume. Knowing my Cousin Inga from a lifetime of correspondence, I was aware that she and I are of similar proportions. Inga would have served as a draper's model in my stead, and a lovely gown would await me. Of this I was certain.

I passed from wakefulness into the land of sleep without being aware of the transition, and dreamed pleasantly of the experiences that lay ahead of me in the company of the wonderful cousin whom I had known all my life through the medium of correspondence but whom I had yet to meet *in propria persona*.

The morning of our planned arrival in New York dawned hot, with a brilliant sun, a lovely blue sky, and even a great white albatross circling above our ship, the traditional symbol of good luck to all nautical enterprises. I breakfasted in company of my brother and several other members of Maestro Ziegfried's ensemble.

It was, perhaps, indication of nervousness upon my part that I was able to take only a cup of fragrant Indian tea and a half-slice of toast lightly coated with orange marmalade for my meal. Need I describe the quantity of scrambled eggs, the slab of broiled ham, the potatoes and biscuits with warm honey which Sherlock consumed, accompanied by a series of cups of rich, steaming hot chocolate *mit schlagsahne.*

My traveling gear was small and so I was able to pack everything into my gripsack quickly enough. I spent the next hour strolling on Oxford Street. At one point I had the misfortune to cross paths with the terrible Mr. Beaufort. Clearly, he recognized me, certainly because of my appearance each night with the *Great*

Eastern's orchestra.

He tipped his hat and offered me one of his metallic smiles. In that moment I felt a chill as I feared that he had penetrated my disguise and recognized me as a member of the female sex. Should this be the case a most unpleasant conversation might all too easily ensue.

But he merely bowed slightly as we passed, walking in opposite directions. 'Mr. Holmes,' he hissed.

'Mr. Beaufort,' I returned.

I walked on as rapidly as I could, hoping that he would not turn and follow me. Fortunately, he did not.

The hours seemed to drag, that day, and yet I was taken by surprise when I realized that night had fallen and it was time for me to repair to my cabin and don my evening outfit.

As is traditional, the last evening of the voyage was observed with a gala dinner. Captain Halpin and his officers were present, each of them wearing his most splendid uniform. The captain's lady and their three daughters were gowned in the most charming fashion. The passengers who filled the salon were similarly garbed in their finest.

The meal included cold lobster, roasted squab, lamb chops with fresh mint sauce, baby peas and carven potatoes. Champagne flowed freely. The repast ended with portions of trifle.

Toasts were offered to Her Majesty, to Mr. Disraeli, to the American President, Mr. Grant, and to Vice President Wilson. A special toast was offered, to the memory of the great Isambard Kingdom Brunel. A resolution of thanks to Captain Halpin and his officers and crew was proposed and adopted by unanimous acclamation of the passengers.

Maestro Ziegfried's orchestra performed a series of numbers alternately stirring and amusing. Our American passengers were clearly pleased to hear the jaunty 'Carve Dat Possum,' by Messers. Lucas and Hershey. A great cheer greeted the 'Water Music' of George Frideric Handel. The Maestro had chosen to end the program with a salute to the United States of America and to our own blessed isle. Alas, the

Americans have no accepted national song. Many of them, I have been led to understand, enjoy singing a set of lyrics by the poet F. S. Key, set to the tune of the 'Anacreontic Song,' but those very words are deemed to be anti-British. Instead, there was an instrumental rendering of their so-called 'Battle Hymn of the Republic,' a reminder of their own Civil War.

At last came the great moment, the orchestral rendering of our own glorious anthem. For this occasion the Maestro elected to add his pianistic talents to those of the rest of the orchestra, whilst conducting, as the expression has it, 'from the keyboard.' All present, further, were invited to give voice to the patriotic words.

Throughout the evening I had cast an occasional glance at Mr. John Gaunt Beaufort, the man of the gleaming teeth. He had drunk a great deal, this much was obvious, but to this moment had behaved himself in an acceptable manner.

All rose.

Maestro raised his hand in signal and the first notes rang out stirringly.

I could see Mr. Beaufort leave his party

and stumble drunkenly toward the front of the grand salon. He climbed clumsily onto the vacant conductor's podium and began to wave his arms as if conducting the orchestra.

Four hundred voices rang out:
God save our gracious Queen,
Long live our noble Queen,
God save the Queen.

Mr. Beaufort reached inside his evening jacket and drew an old-style, two-barreled pistol. He pointed it upward and fired. Stained glass, red, green, golden, purple rained down into the salon.

Half the orchestra ceased playing. Half the room ceased to sing. The other half, perhaps unaware of what had transpired, perhaps too stunned by the suddenness of Beaufort's act, played or sang on:
Send her victorious,
Happy and glorious,
Long to reign over us.

Beaufort lowered his pistol, and pointed it before him. He shouted, 'Deo, regi, patria! Bow before your rightful monarch, Richard the fourth, Rex Anglorum!'

Mr. Albert Saxe, our trumpeter, stood forward, his massive chest expanded like the breast of a pouter pigeon. He spread his arms, the salon's lights glinting from his silver trumpet. 'Shoot,' he commanded, 'if you must. I am your target. Aim well!'

But the delay had given Sherlock time to raise his fiddle and bow, and I, my flute. At his grotesque signal I breathed into the air-hole of my instrument, and he drew his bow across the strings of his. The two sounds converged upon Mr. John Gaunt Beaufort. He screamed in pain and tossed his pistol into the air. As it crashed to the parquet he tumbled from the conductor's dais and rolled on the floor, clutching his jaw in agony as smoke rose from his mouth.

In moments he had been seized by crewmen and hustled from the room, to end the voyage in irons, as he well deserved.

An hour later I sat upon my bunk, trembling. I had decided to end my charade a day early and was garbed in comfortable female costume. Sherlock had doffed his performer's finery and donned his tweeds.

There was a knock upon the door. Sherlock rose and answered it. Standing in the doorway we beheld the rose-cheeked Mr. Jenkins, my fellow flautist. He nodded, smiling, and said, 'Mr. Holmes, and' — he hesitated but for a moment — 'may I presume, Miss Holmes. Would you be so kind as to accompany me.'

Mr. Jenkins offered no explanation, but there was something in his manner that persuaded my brother and myself to comply.

Without further speech we accompanied Mr. Jenkins to a suite guarded by two armed ship's officers. At Mr. Jenkins' knock the door was opened and we were ushered into the presence of two bearded, portly gentlemen, remarkably similar in appearance. One was Captain Robert Halpin, master of the *Great Eastern*. The other was Mr. Albert Saxe, the talented trumpet player.

Mr. Jenkins addressed the latter personage. 'Your Highness, may I present

Mr. Sherlock Holmes and Miss Holmes.'

'Elisabeth, please,' I corrected.

Sherlock and I were in the presence of none other than the Prince of Wales, the Heir Apparent to Victoria's throne. Sharing the suite were Mrs. Halpin and the three Misses Halpin, and a woman whom I recognized as a leading beauty of the London stage.

The Prince shook Sherlock's hand heartily, then reached and embraced me in his great arms. I was bereft of words.

'How can I thank you both,' His Highness said. 'My equerry, whom you know as Mr. Jenkins, was kind enough to tell me who you both are. Your courage and resourcefulness are quite amazing.'

Not one to hold his tongue at a moment like this, Sherlock asked, 'Who was that drunken fool, Your Highness?'

The prince uttered half a laugh, then became more serious. 'Apparently he is a Plantagenet pretender.'

'A criminal!' Sherlock expostulated.

'Perhaps,' said the Prince. 'Or more likely a madman. It is not for me to say. Everything will be sorted out in due course, I am certain.' He issued a sigh. 'I wish I could reward you both suitably but at the moment I am traveling incognito and any ceremony would be unsuitable. But when we return to England, rest assured, I will be in touch with you.'

Sherlock scrabbled in his tweed jacket for pencil and paper. 'Here, Your Highness, I'll give you the address.'

The Prince waved his hand. 'No need. No need, young man. I well know your older brother.'

Two

The Chevalier
C. Auguste Dupin

'It is simple enough as you explain it,' I said, smiling. 'You remind me of Edgar Allan Poe's Dupin. I had no idea that such individuals did exist outside of stories.'

Sherlock Holmes rose and lit his pipe. 'No doubt you think that you are complimenting me in comparing me to Dupin,' he observed. 'Now, in my opinion, Dupin was a very inferior fellow. That trick of his of breaking in on his friends' thoughts with an apropos remark after a quarter of an hour's silence is really very showy and superficial. He had some analytical genius, no doubt; but he was by no means such a phenomenon as Poe appeared to imagine.'

— *A Study in Scarlet*

The Incident of
The Impecunious Chevalier

It was not by choice but by necessity that I continued to read by oil lamp rather than arranging for the installation of the new gas lighting. In my wanderings throughout the metropolis I had been present at demonstrations of M. Lebon's wondrous invention and especially of the improved thorium and cerium mantle devised by Herr von Welsbach, and thought at length of the pleasure of this brilliant mode of illumination, but the undernourished condition of my purse forbad me to pursue such an alteration in the condition of my lodgings.

Even so, I took comfort of an evening in crouching beside the hearth in my lodgings, a small flame of dried driftwood flickering on the stones, a lamp at my elbow, and a volume in my lap. The pleasures of old age are few and small, nor did I anticipate to experience them for many more months before departing this planet and its life of travail. What fate my Maker might plan for me, once my eyes should close for the last time, I could only wonder and await. The priests might assert that a Day of Judgment awaited. The Theosophists might maintain that the doctrine of Karma would apply to all beings. As for me, the Parisian metropolis and its varied denizens were world enough indeed.

My attention had drifted from the printed page before me and my mind had wandered in the byways of philosophical musings to such an extent that the loud rapping upon my door induced a violent start within my nervous system. My fingers relaxed their grasp upon the book which they held, my eyes opened widely and a loud moan escaped my lips.

With an effort I rose to my feet and made my way through my chill and darkened apartment to answer the summons at the door. I placed myself beside the portal, pulling at the draperies that I kept drawn by day against the inquiring gaze of strangers and by night against the moist chill of the Parisian winter. Outside my door I perceived an urchin, cap set at an uncouth angle upon his unshorn head, an object or scrap of material clutched in the hand which he was not using to set up his racket on my door.

Lifting an iron bar which I kept beside the door in case of need to defend myself from the invasion of ruffians and setting the latch chain to prevent the door from opening more than a hand's width, I turned the latch and drew the door open far enough to peer out.

The boy who stood upon my stoop could not have been more than ten years of age, ragged of clothing and filthy of visage. The meager light of the passage outside my apartment reflected from his eye, giving an impression of wary suspicion. We studied each other through the narrow opening for long seconds before either spoke. At length I demanded to know his reason for disturbing my musings. He ignored my question, responding to it by speaking my name.

'Yes,' I responded, 'it is indeed I. Again,

I require to know the purpose of your visit.'

'I've brought you a message, monsieur,' the urchin stated.

'From whom?'

'I don't know the gentleman's name,' he replied.

'Then what is the message?'

The boy held the object in his hand closer to the opening. I could see now that it was a letter, folded and sealed with wax, and crumpled and covered with grime. It struck me that the boy might have found the paper lying in a gutter and brought it to me as part of a devious scheme, but then I remembered that he had known my name, a feat not likely on the part of a wild street urchin.

'I can't read, monsieur,' the child said. 'The gentleman gave it me and directed me to your lodging. I know numbers, some, and was able to find your place, monsieur.'

'Very well,' I assented, 'give me the paper.'

'I've got to be paid first, monsieur.'

The boy's demand was annoying, and

yet he had performed a service and was, I suppose, entitled to his pay. Perhaps the mysterious gentleman who had dispatched him had already furnished him with payment, but this was a contingency beyond my ability to influence. Telling the child to await my return I closed the door, made my way to the place where I keep my small treasury, and extracted from it a sou coin.

At the doorway once more I exchanged the coin for the paper and sent the child on his way. Returning to the dual illumination of hearth and oil lamp, I broke the seal that held the letter closed and unfolded the sheet of foolscap. The flickering firelight revealed to me the work of a familiar hand, albeit one I had not glimpsed for many years, and a message that was characteristically terse and demanding. *Come at once. A matter of urgency.* The message was signed with a single letter, the initial *D*. I rocked back upon my heels, sinking into the old chair which I had used as my comfort and my retreat from the world through the passing decades. I was clad in slippers and robe, nightcap perched upon my head. It has been my plan, following a small meal, to spend an hour reading and then to retire to my narrow bed. Instead, I now garbed myself for the chill of the out-of-doors. Again I raided my own poor treasury and furnished myself with a small reserve of coins. In a short time I had left my apartment and stood upon my stoop, drawing behind me the doorway and turning my key in the lock.

No address had been given in the demanding message, nor was the messenger anywhere to be seen. I could only infer from the lack of information to the contrary that my old friend was still to be located at the lodgings we once had shared, long ago.

It was too far to travel on foot, so I hailed a passing cab, not without difficulty, and instructed the driver as to my destination. He looked at me with suspicion until I repeated the address, 33 Rue Dunot in the Faubourg St-Germain. He held out his hand and refused to whip up until I had delivered the fare into his possession.

The streets of the metropolis were deserted at this hour, and mostly silent save for an occasional shout of anger or moan of despair — the sounds of the night after even revelers have retired to their homes or elsewhere.

As the cab drew up I exited from it and stood gazing at the old stone structure where the two of us had shared quarters for so long. Behind me I heard the driver grumble, then whip up, then pull away from number 33 with the creak of the wooden axle and the clatter of horse's hooves on cobblestones.

A light appeared in a window and I tried, without success, to espy the form of the person who held it. In a moment the light moved and I knew that my erstwhile friend was making his way to the door. I presented myself in time to hear the bar withdrawn and to see the door swing open.

Before me stood my old friend, the world's first and greatest consulting detective, the Chevalier C. Auguste Dupin. Yet though it was unquestionably he, I was shocked at the ravages that the years had worked upon his once sharp-featured visage and whip-thin frame. He had grown old. The flesh did not so much cover his bones as hang from them. I saw that he still wore the smoked-glass spectacles of an earlier age; when he raised them to peer at me his once ferret-like eyes were dim and his hands, once as hard and steady as iron rods, appeared fragile and tremulous.

'Do not stand there like a goose,' Dupin commanded, 'surely by this time you know the way.'

He retreated a pace and I entered the apartment which had meant so much to me in those days of our companionship. Characteristically, Dupin uttered not another syllable, but instead led the way through my onetime home. I shut the door behind me, then threw the heavy iron bolt, mindful of the enemies known to seek Dupin's destruction in a former epoch. That any of them still survived was doubtful, that they remained capable of working mischief upon the great mind was close to what Dupin would have deemed 'a nil possibility,' but still I threw the bolt.

Dupin led the way to his book closet, and within moments it was almost as if the decades had slipped away. He seemed to regain his youthful vigor, and I my former enthusiasm. Not waiting for me to assume the sofa upon which I had so often reclined to peruse musty volumes in past decades Dupin flung himself into his favorite seat. He seized a volume which he had laid face downward, its pages open, upon the arm of his chair.

'Have you seen this?' he demanded angrily, brandishing the volume.

I leaned forward, straining in the gloom to recognize the publication. 'It bears no familiarity,' I confessed. 'It looks but newly arrived, and my reading in recent years has been entirely of an antiquarian nature.'

'Of course, of course,' Dupin muttered. 'I will tell you what it is. I have been reading a volume translated from the English. Its title in our own tongue is *Une Étude en écarlate*. The author has divided the work into chapters. I will read to you from a chapter which he entitles ingenuously *La Science de déduction*.

Knowing that there was no stopping Dupin once he was determined upon a course, I settled upon the sofa. The room was not uncomfortable, I was in the company of my ancient friend, I was content.

'I will omit the author's interpolations,' Dupin prefaced his reading, 'and present to you only the significant portions of his work. Very well, then! *Now, in my opinion, Dupin was a very inferior fellow. That trick of his of breaking in on his friends' thoughts with an apropos remark after a quarter of an hour's silence is really very showy and superficial. He had some analytical genius, no doubt; but he was by no means such a phenomenon as Poe appeared to imagine.*

With a furious gesture he flung the slim volume across the room against a shelf of volumes, where it struck, its pages fluttering, and fell to the carpet. I knew that the Poe to whom the writer averred was the American journalist who had visited Dupin and myself from time to time, authoring reports of the several mysteries which Dupin had unraveled with, I took pride in recalling, my own modest but not insubstantial assistance.

'What think you of that?' Dupin demanded.

'A cruel assessment,' I ventured, 'and an inaccurate one. Why, on many occasions I can recall — '

'Indeed, my good friend, you can recall the occasions upon which I interrupted your words to tell you your very thoughts.'

'As you have just done,' I averred. I awaited further words from Dupin, but they were not at that moment forthcoming so I resumed my speech. 'Who is the author of this scurrilous assessment?'

'The author's name matters not. It is the villain whom he quotes, who is of significance.'

'And who, may I inquire, might that person be?'

Dupin raised his eyes to the ceiling where smoke from the fireplace, draughty as ever, swirled menacingly. 'He is one whom I met some years ago, long after you had departed these quarters, *mon ami*. I had by then largely retired from my labors as a consulting detective, and of course my reputation had long since reached the islands of fools.'

By this time I could see that Dupin was off on a tale, and I settled myself more thoroughly than ever upon the sofa, prepared to listen to the end:

Those were days of tumult in our nation (Dupin said) when danger lurked at every turning and the most ordinary of municipal services were not to be taken for granted. When I received a message from across the Channel, I was of course intrigued.

The writer was a young man who professed admiration for my exploits and a desire to learn my methods that he might emulate them in the building of a reputation and a career for himself in his own land. I received many such communications in those days, responding to them uniformly that the entire science of detection was but a matter of observation and deduction, and that any man or even woman of ordinary intelligence could match my feats did he or she but apply those faculties with which we are all equipped to their full capacity. But the person who had written to me mentioned a particular case which he had been employed to resolve, and when he described the case my curiosity was piqued.

Your expression tells me that you, too, are aroused by the prospect of this case, and I will tell you what it concerned.

The young man's letter of application hinted only of a treasure of fabulous value, a cache of gold and gems lost some three centuries, that had become the subject of legend and of fanciful tales, but which he believed to exist in actuality and to be in France, nay, not merely in France but in the environs of Paris itself. Could he but find it he would be wealthy beyond the power of imagination, and if I would but assist him in his quest a portion of it would be mine.

As you know, while I am of good family I have long been of reduced means, and the prospect of restoring the fortunes of my forebears was an attractive one. My correspondent was reticent as to details in his letters, for I wrote back to him seeking further information but was unable to elicit useful data.

At length I permitted him to visit me — yes, in this very apartment. From the first his eccentric nature was manifest. He arrived at a late hour, as late I daresay as you have yourself arrived this night. It was the night before that of the full moon. The air was clear and the sky filled with celestial objects whose illumination, added to that of the moon, approached that of the day.

He sat upon the very sofa where you recline at this moment. No, there is no need to rise and examine the furnishing. You do make me smile, old friend. There is nothing to be learned from that old sofa.

The young man, an Englishman, was of tall and muscular build with a hawk-like visage, sharp features, and a sharp, observant mien. His clothing bore the strong odor of tobacco. His hollow eyes suggested his habituation to some stronger stimulant. His movements suggested one who has trained in the boxing ring; more, one who has at least familiarized himself with the Japanese art of *baritsu*, a subtle form of combat but recently introduced in a few secretive salons in Paris and Berlin, in London, and even in the city of Baltimore in Maryland.

It took me but moments to realize that this was a person of unusual talent, potentially a practitioner of the craft of detection to approach my own level of proficiency. It was obvious to me as we conversed on this topic and that, the politics of our respective nations, the growing incidence of crime which respects neither border nor sea, the advances of science and literature among the Gallic and Anglic races, that he was watching me closely, attempting to draw my measure even as I was, his.

At length, feeling that I had seen all that he would reveal of himself, and growing impatient with his avoidance of the topic that had drawn him to my apartments, I demanded once for all that he describe that which he sought and in the recovery of which he desired my guidance, or else depart from my lodging, having provided me with an hour's diversion and no more.

'Very well, sir,' he replied, 'I will tell

you that I am in search of a bird.'

Upon his making this statement I burst into laughter, only to be shocked back to sobriety by the stern expression upon the face of my visitor. 'Surely, sir,' I exclaimed, 'you did not brave the stormy waters of the Channel in search of a grouse or guinea hen.'

'No, sir,' he replied, 'I have come in search of a plain black bird, a bird variously described in the literature as a raven or, more likely, a hawk.'

'The feathers of hawks are not black,' I replied.

'Indeed, sir, you are correct. The feathers of hawks are not black, nor has this hawk feathers of any color, but the color of this hawk is golden.'

'You insult me, sir,' I stated angrily.

My visitor raised his eyebrows. 'Why say you so?'

'You come to me and speak only in riddles, as if you were humoring a playful child. A hawk that is black but has no feathers and yet is golden. If you do not make yourself more clear you must leave my apartments, and I wish you a speedy return to your country.'

He raised a hand placatingly. 'I did not wish to offend you, sir, nor to speak in conundrums. Pray, bear with me for a little longer and I will make clear the nature and history of the odd bird which I seek.'

I permitted him to continue.

'This was the representation of a bird,' quoth he, 'the creation of a group of talented metalworkers and gemsmiths, Turkish slaves employed by the Grand Master Villiers de L'Isle Adam, of the Order of the Knights of Rhodes. It was crafted in the year 1530, and dispatched by galley from the Isles of Rhodes to Spain, where it was to be presented to the Emperor Charles the Fifth. Its height was as the length of your forearm. It was of solid gold, in the form of a standing hawk or raven, and it was crusted over with gems of the greatest variety and finest quality. Its value even at the time was immense. Today it would be incalculable!'

He paused, a look in his eyes as if he could envision the fantastic sight of a golden falcon, emeralds for its eyes and rubies for its claws, circling the chamber. Then he resumed his narrative.

He then did something which seemed, at the moment, very peculiar but which, I would come to realize, was in truth to have been expected of a man such as he. He leaped from his seat upon the cushion and began pacing restlessly around the chamber. At once I inquired as to what had caused such an abrupt alteration in his manner and demeanor, whereupon he turned upon me a visage transformed. The muscles of his face were drawn, his lips were pulled back to expose gleaming teeth, and his eyes, by heaven, his eyes glittered like the eyes of a wild leopard.

'I must visit an apothecary at once,' he exclaimed.

In response to this demand I remonstrated with him. 'Sir, there is an excellent apothecary shop upon the Rue Dunot, an easy walk from here, but what is the urgency? A moment ago you were calmly describing a most extraordinary bird. Now you demand directions to the establishment of a chemist.'

'It will pass,' he responded, most

puzzlingly, 'it will pass.'

He sank once more to his former position upon the sofa and, pressing the heels of his hands to his deep-sunken eyes, paused to draw a deep breath.

'Do you wish to continue?' I inquired.

'Yes, yes. But if you would be so kind, monsieur, as to furnish me with a glass of wine, I would be most grateful.'

I rose and proceeded to the wine cupboard, from which I drew a dust-coated bottle of my second-best vintage. In those days as in these, as you are of course aware, I saw fit to maintain my own household, without benefit of servant or staff. I poured a glass for my guest and he tossed it off as one would a draught of water, extending the emptied goblet for a second portion, which I forthwith poured. This he studied, lifted to his lips and sipped, then placed carefully upon the taboret before him.

'Do you wish to continue your narration?' I inquired.

'If you please,' he responded, 'I beg your indulgence for my outburst. I am not, I must confess, entirely well.'

'Should the need arise,' I assured him, 'M. Konstantinides, the chemist, is qualified to provide specifics for all known illnesses. The hour is late and he would by now have closed his establishment for the night and retired to his chamber, but I could rouse him in your behalf.'

'You are gracious, sir. I trust that will prove unnecessary, but I am nonetheless grateful.' Once more he paused as if to gather his thoughts, then launched upon a further exposition. 'I will not trouble you with every detail of the peregrinations of the golden falcon, save to point out that within our own generation it had passed into the possession of the Carlist movement in Spain.'

To this statement I nodded. 'Wars of succession are tiresome, but it seems they will be with us always, does it not? I was struck by the recent surrender of Señor Maroto's Basque followers after their lengthy and strenuous resistance.'

'You are well informed, sir! If you are familiar with the fate of the Basque Carlists, then you would know that Señor

Ramon Cabrera has continued the struggle in Catalonia.'

'He is also in dire straits, is he not?'

'Yes, it appears that Her Majesty Isabella the Second is at last about to reap the harvest of the Salic Law invoked by her royal father. But I fear I am boring you, M. Dupin.'

'Not so much boring as stimulating my curiosity. Surely, sir, you did not travel here from London merely to relate the saga of a fabulous bird and then digress upon the politics of the Spanish succession. How are these things related, for surely that must be the case. If you would be so kind as to come to the point, then.'

'Indeed.' He bowed his head, then raised it once more. 'You are aware, surely, that Don Carlos has sympathizers here in France. You were perhaps not aware that Señor Cabrera had sent an agent on a dangerous and secretive mission, to traverse the passes of the Pyrenees and make his way to the château of a French sympathizer, no less a personage than the Duc de Lagny.'

'I am familiar with Lagny,' I confessed.

'I have had the pleasure of being introduced to His Grace and to Her Grace the Duchess. Their château is of noteworthy architecture. But of the Duke's Carlist sympathies I must confess profound ignorance.

'That is not surprising, sir. The Duke is known, if I may make a small play on words, for his reclusiveness.'

He paused to sip once more at his, or perhaps I should say, my, wine. 'Regarding the golden bird as an omen and token of majesty, and sensing the imminent defeat of the Carlist cause, Senor Cabrera had sent the bird to Lagny rather than have it fall into the hands of his niece's followers.'

'And you wish me to assist you in retrieving the bird from the château of the Duc de Lagny?' I asked.

'That is my mission.'

'You are in the employ of Her Majesty Isabella?'

'I am in the employ of one whose identity I am not at liberty to disclose.' He rose to his feet. 'If you will assist me — for my knowledge of the French countryside and culture is limited — you will receive, shall I say, sir, a reward of royal proportions.'

'You wish me to accompany you to the château of the Duke,' I objected, 'there to obtain from his custody the fabled bird. What causes you to believe that he will relinquish it?'

'You have my assurance, monsieur, the Duke will be eager to part with that which he safeguards upon receiving proof of the identity of my employers.'

'You have such proof with you?' I demanded.

'I have, sir,' he insisted. 'Upon this fact I give you my solemn assurance.'

Unable to deny an interest in obtaining a share of the lucre to which he referred, and perhaps attracted to an extent by the lure of the romantic story he had spun, I agreed, at the least, to accompany him to Lagny. I have told you already that the hour of my guest's arrival was an unconventionally late one, and his dis-quisitive manner of speech had caused the hours to pass before our bargain, such as it might be, was struck.

At length I excused myself and proceeded to the front parlor of my apartment. The act of drawing back the draperies confirmed that which I had already suspected, namely, that dawn had broken and a new day was upon us. Feeling impelled to violate my custom and venture forth from my lodgings in the light of day, I urged my visitor to the stoop, drew shut the door behind us, and locked it. We set out on foot to the apothecary shop of M. Konstantinides. Here my guest purchased a preparation and induced it into his own system.

I was by no means unfamiliar with the effects of various stimulants and depressants upon the human organism, but even so I will own that I was startled at the strength and portion taken by this nearly skeletal Englishman. At once his air of distress left him and his visage assumed an altogether more friendly and optimistic appearance than had previously been the case. He paid M. Konstantinides his fee, adding a generous overage thereto, and then, turning to me, suggested that we set out for Lagny.

Our journey was not a difficult one. We hired a hackney carriage and negotiated a fare all the way to the village of Lagny, the sum being paid from my guest's purse, and proceeded eastward from the capital. It was necessary to pause but once at an inn, where we procured a loaf, a cheese, and bottle, my English guest and I dining in democratic fashion with the hackman.

The sun drew low in the sky behind us as we approached Lagny. I was able, by drawing upon my memory of earlier days, to direct the hackman past the village to the château of the Duke. It was a tall and rambling structure of ancient Gothic construction; as we neared the château the sun's guttering rays painted its walls as if with a palette of flame. We debouched from the carriage and instructed the hackman to return to the village and to return for us in the morning.

He asked in his rude yet charmingly colorful way, 'And who's to pay for me sups and me snooze, ye two toffs?'

'We shall indeed,' my English guest responded, dropping a handful of coins onto the coach box, upon which the hackman whipped up and departed.

The Château de Lagny, if I may so describe it, radiated an air of age and decadence. As my guest and I stood gazing at its façade he turned to me and asked a peculiar question. 'What do you hear, my dear Dupin?'

Perhaps I ought to have taken offense at this unwonted familiarity, but instead I chose to deal with his query. I cocked an ear, gave list carefully to whatever sounds there might be emanating from the château, then made my reply. 'I hear nothing.'

'Precisely!' the Englishman exclaimed.

'And what, sir, is the object of this schoolmasterly exchange?' I inquired.

'Sir — ' He smiled. ' — would one not expect to hear the bustle of life in such a setting as this? The neigh of horses from the stables, the cry of servants and workers, mayhap the sound of revelers? None of this, I repeat, none of it do we hear. Only a silence, M. Dupin, only an eerie, deathlike silence.'

For once I was forced to concede that my visitor had scored a point upon me. I acknowledged as much, to which he perhaps grudgingly conceded that I was yet the master and he the eager pupil. He refrained from commenting upon the looming day when the pupil might outstrip the master in achievement, nor was I prepared to do so.

Arm in arm we approached the main entryway of the château. We carried, of course, walking sticks, and I permitted my companion to raise his and strike heavily upon the great wooden door. To my astonishment no servant appeared to grant us entry. Instead, the door swung slowly open and the two of us set foot upon the flagging on the château's foyer.

At first nothing appeared out of the way, but in moments our nostrils were assailed by the unmistakable odor of decomposition. Exchanging glances but not a word, we drew kerchiefs from our respective pockets and knotted them over our nostrils and mouths. I turned toward my companion and observed him, hatted and masked like a highwayman. Full well I knew that my own appearance was as sinister as his.

The first cadaver we encountered was that of a liveried footman. First instructing my guest to maintain careful watch lest violence appear from within the château, I knelt over the still form. Had the stench not been evidence enough of death, the condition of the footman's body would have fully convinced the veriest of laymen. He had been struck down from behind. He lay upon his face, the back of his head crushed, the pooled gore already beginning to crawl with insects.

Turning aside to draw a breath of clear air, or at any rate of air more clear than that surrounding the cadaver, I examined the clothing of the deceased in search of a clue as to the motive for his murder, but discovered nothing.

Proceeding through the house my associate and I found, in turn, the remains of maids, cooks, laundresses, and an elderly male servant whom we took to be the major-domo of the establishment. But what had happened, and where was the master of the château?

Him we found in the stables behind the

château. Surrounded by stablemen lay M. le Duc. The hearty nobleman whose company I had enjoyed more than once had been treated disgustingly. It was obvious from the condition of the remains that the Duke had been tortured. His hands were bound behind his back and his face showed the discolorations caused by the application of a heated implement. Surely the intention had been to force from him the location of the fabled golden bird. Marks upon his torso were enough to sicken the viewer, while the final, fatal attack had come in the form of a sharpened blade drawn across his belly, exposing his vital organs and inducing the ultimate exsanguination.

Her Grace the Duchess had been treated in similar fashion. I will not describe the indignities which had been visited upon her. One prayed only that her more delicate frame had reached its limits and that she had been granted the mercy of a death more rapid and less agonizing that that of her husband.

Horses and dogs, like the human inhabitants of the estate, lay at random, slaughtered every one.

'Is this the work of Señor Cabrera and his men?' I asked.

'More likely of the servants of Isabella,' my guest replied. 'The deaths of these unfortunate persons and their beasts are to be regretted, but of immediate concern is the whereabouts of the bird.' He stood over first one cadaver, then another, studying them as would a student of medicine the dissected remains of a beast.

'It appears unlikely that the secret was divulged,' he suggested at length. 'Obviously the Duke was tortured and dispatched first, for such a nobleman as he would not have permitted his lady to be treated as we see her to have been. Nor, I would infer, did the Duchess know the whereabouts of the bird, for once her husband was deceased, she would have had no reason to protect the secret. On the contrary, having presumably seen her attackers, she would have sought to survive in order to exact revenge for the murder of her husband.'

His callous attitude toward the carnage we had only just beheld was appalling, but then the English are known to be a cold-blooded race, and it may be that this Englishman felt a degree of sympathy and outrage that he did not show. Very well, then. When the hackman returned for us on the morrow, I would inform the mayor of the village of Lagny of our terrible discovery. The brutal criminals responsible would be sought and, one hoped, brought to face their fate beneath the guillotine in due course. But my guest was right, at least to the extent that our own presence at the Château de Lagny had been brought about by the report of the presence of the bird.

We would seek it, and if it was here, I knew that we would find it.

'Let us proceed to locate the golden bird,' I announced to my guest. 'So splendid an object should be conspicuous to the eye of anyone save a blind man.'

'Perhaps not,' the Englishman demurred. 'I will confess, my dear Dupin, that I have withheld from you one item in the history and description of the bird.'

I demanded that he enlighten me at once, and in what for him passed for a direct response, he complied. 'You have doubtlessly noticed that in my descriptions of the bird I have referred to it both as golden and as black.'

'I have done so, sir. You may in fact recall my bringing this discrepancy to your attention, and your pledge to reconcile the conflicting descriptions. If you please, this would seem an excellent time to do so.'

'Very well, then. The bird as originally created by the captive Turkish craftsmen, of solid gold virtually encrusted with precious stones, was considered too attractive a target. At some point in its history — I confess to ignorance of the exact date — it was coated in a black substance, a thick, tarry pigment, so that it now resembles nothing more than a sculpture of ebony in the form of a standing hawk.'

'What leads you to believe that the bird is still in the château? Even if the Duke and Duchess died without revealing the secret of its hiding place to their enemies, those villains might still have searched the château until they found the bird. But look about you, sir, and you will see that we are surrounded by a scene not merely of carnage, but of despoliation. It is obvious that the château has been ransacked. You did not yourself know of the bird's hiding place? Your employers did not inform you?'

'My employers did not themselves know the hiding place. It was the Duke himself who chose that, after the messengers had left.'

'Then for all we know, the bird has flown.'

'No, sir.' The Englishman shook his head. 'By the condition of the bodies, even in winter, this horror occurred at least four days ago, before I left London. I would have received word, had the villains succeeded. They have committed these horrendous crimes in vain. You may rest assured that the bird is still here. But where?'

'Let us consider,' I suggested. 'The interior of the château and even, to the extent that we have searched, of the outbuildings, have been torn apart. Furniture is demolished, pictures and tapestries torn from walls. The Duke's library has been despoiled, his priceless collection of ancient manuscripts and rare volumes reduced to worthless rubble. Even a suit of ancient armor has been thrown from its stand so that it lies in pieces upon the flagging. The invaders of the château may be monsters, but they are not unintelligent nor yet are they lacking in thoroughness.'

I paused, awaiting further comment by the Englishman, but none was forthcoming. I observed him closely and perceived that he was perspiring freely and that he alternately clenched and loosened his fists almost as one suffering a fit.

'If the bird is still on the estate,' I resumed, 'yet it is not within the château or its outbuildings, logic dictates its location to us. Consider this, young man. We have eliminated the partial contents of our list of possibilities. Having done so, we are drawn irresistibly to the conclusion that the remaining possibilities must contain the solution to our puzzle. Do you follow the thread of ratiocination which I have laid before you?'

He seemed to relax, as if the fit had passed. He drew a cloth from a pocket of his costume and wiped the perspiration from his brow. He acknowledged the irrefutable nature of my argument.

'But,' he continued, 'I fail to see the next step in your procedure.'

'You disappoint me,' I uttered. 'Very well. If you will please follow me.' I retreated to the main entry hall of the château, and thence to the terrace outside. I proceeded still farther, my boots leaving a trail behind me in the heavy dew that had accumulated upon the lush lawn surrounding the château. The moon had attained fullness, and the sky above Lagny was even more impressive than that above the metropolis had been.

'Do you look upon the château,' I instructed my pupil, for I had so come to regard the Englishman.

He stood beside me and gazed at the structure, its stone pediments rendered in pale chiaroscuro by the light streaming from the heavens. 'What see you?' I asked him. 'Why, the Château de Lagny,' he replied at once. 'Indeed. What else do you see?'

The young Englishman pursed his lips with the appearance of impatience. 'Only that, sir. The stable and other outbuildings are concealed by the bulk of the château.'

'Indeed,' I nodded. I spoke no more, awaiting further comment by the other. There ensued a lengthy silence.

Finally, in a tone of impatience, my student spoke once more. 'The lawn before the château. The woods which surround us. The moon, the stars. A tiny cloud in the southwest.'

I nodded. 'Very good. More.'

'For the love of God, Dupin, what more is there to see?'

'Only that which is vital to our mission,' I replied.

As I watched, the Englishman raised his eyes once more, then froze. 'I see a row of birds perched upon the parapet of the château.'

'My good fellow!' I exclaimed, 'it appears now possible that you may have the makings of a detective. Further, I urge you, do not satisfy yourself with merely seeing, but observe, observe, observe, and report!'

He stood silent and motionless for some time, then took an action which won my admiration. Although we stood ankle-deep in the dew-soaked grass before the château, there was nearby a driveway used by carriages approaching and departing the estate. Our own cabman had followed this path, and it was my expectation that he would utilize it once more upon his return for us in the morning.

The Englishman strode to the driveway, bent, and lifted a handful of gravel. He threw back his cape so as to free his arm and flung the gravel at the birds perched upon the parapet. I was impressed by the strength and accuracy of his arm.

With an angry outcry several of the birds flew from their perch. They were silhouetted against the night sky, their form limned in a drab black against the glittering stars and clear darkness of the heavens. One of them passed across the face of the full, brilliant moon, its widespread wings and the shining disk behind it creating the illusion that the bird was as large as the legendary Pegasus.

My student and I remained motionless, observing the behavior of the aerial creatures. They were more annoyed than frightened by the clattering pebbles, or so I inferred, for it took mere moments for the plurality of the creatures to return to their former places, midst an audible flapping of feathery wings and grumbling calls.

The Englishman bent and lifted another handful of gravel, drew back his arm and flung the stones at the birds. Once more his action evoked an angry response, most of the birds crying out in annoyance and flapping away from their perch. By now the solution to the mystery of the missing hawk was apparent.

'Good work,' I congratulated my student. 'It is clear that you have grasped the difference between observing and merely seeing, and have observed that which is necessary to locate your prey.'

A small indication of pleasure made

itself visible upon his face, the momentary upward twitching of the corners of his mouth by a few millimeters. Without uttering a word he seated himself upon the grass and proceeded to remove his boots and stockings. I watched in equal silence as he strode to the outer wall of the château.

It has been my expectation that he would return to the interior of the structure and seek access to the roof by means of interior staircases. Instead, to my amazement, after studying the wall with its closely fitted stones and creeping ivy, he proceeded to climb the exterior of the château, using his powerful fingers and almost orang-utan-like toes to assure his grasp. As he advanced his cape flapped about his form like two huge wings.

As he approached the parapet he called out to the winged creatures perched there, making a peculiar sound unlike any I had previously heard. Without preliminary, the avians watching his advance extended their wings and rose from the château, disappearing into the blackness that surrounded them. All save one. A single bird remained stationary, silhouetted against the starry domain.

The strange, almost inhuman, being into which my erstwhile visitor had transformed himself, perched now beside the sole remaining avian, so high above the earth that a single slip, I could see, would plunge him to a certain doom. Yet no sound reached me from this strange personage, nor any indication of fear.

He lifted the unmoving bird from its place and in a moment it disappeared beneath his cloak. I could only infer that he had come prepared with an extra section of leather belting or rope, concealed until now by his outer garments.

Then as I stood aghast he lowered himself to lie flat upon the parapet, then reached over its edge to gain a handhold on the stone wall, then slid from his safe perch and proceeded to climb down the wall of the château, headfirst, the bird secured beneath his clothing. His appearance, for all the world, was that of a gigantic bat.

When he reached the greensward he righted himself and drew the bird from beneath his cape. 'I thank you, my dear Dupin, for the lessons you have given me, equally in observation and in deduction. Our prey is recovered.'

So saying he held the black bird toward me. Even through its black coating I could make out the shape of its feathers, its claws, its beak and its eyes. It was clearly a magnificent example of the sculptor's art. My student asked me to hold the figurine while he once more donned his stockings and boots. The weight of the black bird was so great that I felt even greater astonishment at his ability to descend the wall of the château with it strapped beneath his clothing.

We spent what little remained of the night exploring the interior of the château, utilizing torches which remained from that sad structure's happier era. The only clues that we uncovered were further evidence of the brutality of the invaders who had slaughtered the Duke and Duchess as well as their retainers, all in a futile attempt to learn the whereabouts of the treasure which my pupil and I now possessed.

With morning our hackman arrived, somewhat the worse for wear and, one inferred, for the consumption of excessive amounts of spirit. I instructed him to take us to the village of Lagny, where we concealed the bird inside the boot of the hack, promising the hackman a generous tip in exchange for his silence. We thereupon made a full report of our gory findings at the château, making no mention of the bird. The reason we gave for our visit to the château was the truthful one that I was an old acquaintance of the Duke and Duchess and had been eager to introduce to them my visitor from England.

The mayor of the village of Lagny and the *chef des gendarmes* were duly horrified by our descriptions, but permitted us to depart for Paris upon our pledge to provide what information and assistance we could, should these be called for at a later stage of their investigation.

In due course the hack pulled up at my lodgings in the Faubourg St.-Germain. A light snow had fallen in the metropolis, and I picked my way carefully to my door lest I slip and fall to the stones. Exhausted by the activities of the past day and night, I turned my key in the lock of my lodgings and pushed the door open so that my guest and I might enter. When we did so we were confronted by an unanticipated sight. My quarters had been ransacked. Furniture was overturned, drawers were pulled from their places and inverted upon the floor. The carpeting had been torn up and rolled back to permit a search for trapdoors or loosened boards.

Every picture was pulled from the wall and thrown to the floor, including that of my friend and idol the great Vidocq. Shocked and offended by the invasion of my quarters I proceeded to examine their contents, assessing the damage and grieving for the destruction of precious mementos of a long career. I clutched my head and expostulated my outrage.

Drawing myself together at length and hoping in some manner to mitigate the harm which had been done I turned to confer with my visitor, only to find that he had disappeared without a trace.

I flew to the doorway and exited my premises. The hack had of course departed long since, but a row of dark footprints showed in the fresh snow. Following without heed to the risk of falling I dashed the length of the Rue Dunot. At length I found myself standing upon the doorstep of the establishment of M. Konstantinides. I sounded the bell repeatedly but without response, then pounded upon the door. Neither light nor movement could be seen from within the shop, nor was there response of any sort to my summons.

At once the meaning of these events burst upon my tortured brain. The Englishman was a dope fiend, the Greek apothecary the supplier of his evil chemicals. How Konstantinides had obtained knowledge of the bird was unfathomable, but it was at his behest rather than that of either the Carlists or the Bourbons that I had been recruited.

Konstantinides had ransacked my lodgings merely as a distraction, to hold my attention while the Englishman brought the bird to his shop. By now, even though mere minutes had passed, it was a certainty that both the Englishman and the Greek, along with the black bird, were gone from the Faubourg and would not be found within the environs of Paris.

What would become of the bird, of the English detective, of the Greek chemist, were mysteries for the years to come. And now at last (Dupin completed his narrative) I learn of the further career of my student, and of the scorn with which he repays my guidance.

As I sat, mortified by my friend and mentor's humiliation, I saw him clutching the small volume from which he had read the cruel words as if it were a dagger with which he planned to take his own life. All the while he had been telling his tale I had been carried away by the narrative, to another time and place, a time and place when Dupin was young and in his prime. But now I had returned to the present and saw before me a man enfeebled by the passage of the years and the exigencies of a cruel existence.

'What became of the bird?' I inquired. 'Did it disappear entirely?'

Dupin shook his head. 'The apothecary shop of the Greek Konstantinides was reopened by a nephew. Of the elder Konstantinides nothing was ever again heard, or if it was, it was held inviolate in the bosom of the family. I attempted to learn from the nephew the whereabouts of his uncle and of the Englishman, as well as of the bird itself, but the younger Konstantinides pled ignorance of the fate of the two men, as well as that the bird. For two generations now the shop has remained in the family, and the secret, if secret there is, remains sealed in their bosom.'

I nodded my understanding. 'And so you never again heard of your pupil, the strange Englishman?'

Dupin waved the book at me. 'You see, old friend? He has become, as it were, the new Dupin. His fame spreads across the seas and around the globe. Did he but make the meanest acknowledgment of his debt to me, I would be satisfied. My material needs are met by the small pension arranged by our old friend G — of the Metropolitan Police Force. My memories are mine, and your own writings have given me my small share of fame.'

'The very least I could do, Dupin, I assure you.'

There followed a melancholy silence during which I contemplated the sad state to which my friend had fallen. At length he heaved a sigh pregnant with despair. 'Perhaps,' he began, then lapsed, then again began, 'perhaps it would be of interest to the discerning few to learn of a few of my other undertakings.'

Shaking my head I responded, 'Already have I recorded them, Dupin. There was the case of the murders in the Rue Morgue, that of the purloined letter, and even your brilliant solution of the mystery of Marie Roget.'

'Those are not the cases to which I refer,' Dupin demurred.

'I know of no others, save, of course that which you have narrated to me this night.'

Upon hearing my words, Dupin permitted himself one of the rarest smiles which I have ever seen upon his countenance.

'There have been many others, dear friend,' he informed me, 'many indeed.'

Astonished, I begged him to enumerate a few such.

'There were the puzzle of the Tsaritsa's false emerald, the adventure of Wade the American gunrunner, the mystery of the Algerian herbs, the incident of the Bahamian fugitive and the runaway hot-air balloon, and of course the tragedy of the pharaoh's jackal.'

'I shall be eager to record these, Dupin. Is the list thus complete?'

'By no means, old friend. That is merely the beginning. Such reports may in some small way assuage the pain of being aged and forgotten, replaced on the stage of detection by a newer generation of sleuths. And, I suspect, the few coins which your reports may add to your purse will not be unwelcome.'

'They will not,' I was forced to concede.

'But this — ' Dupin waved the book once more. ' — this affront strikes to my heart. As bitter as wormwood and as sharp as a two-edged sword, so sayeth the proverb.'

'Dupin,' I said, 'you will not be forgotten. This English prig has clearly copied your methods, even to the degree of enlisting an assistant and amanuensis who bears a certain resemblance to myself. Surely justice forbids that the world forget the Chevalier C. Auguste Dupin!'

'Not forget?' my friend mumbled. 'Not forget? The pupil will live in fame forever while the master becomes but a footnote to the history of detection. Ah, my friend, my dear, dear friend, but the world in which we live is unjust.'

'It was ever thus, Dupin,' I concurred, 'it was ever thus.'

Three

Three

The Case of The Doctor Who Had No Business

or

The Adventure of The Second Anonymous Narrator

The London sky was lowering and a near-black gray on a certain night in mid-November of 1911. A stocky, balding man of thirty-odd years made his way down Pall Mall from the St. James's end, his greatcoat lapels turned up against the precipitation-tainted wind, his ham-like fists buried deep in huge pockets stretched to sack-like proportions by those same strong hands.

The big man paused at a door some little distance from the Carlton, bringing forth from one of those pockets a crumpled telegram which had brought him out of his respectable but somewhat shabby hotel on a night reminiscent of those he had grown used to in his native Chicago, some four thousand miles to the west. Again, his somewhat tired eyes straining against the dim London gas lamps, he read:

If you would learn something of probable interest and possible profit to you, be so kind as to call upon me this evening at my club. It is the Diogenes — the deskman at your hotel will surely provide directions.

Probable interest and possible profit, mused the American as he entered the hall. Possible profit meant certain interest to him with a growing family at home in America, a string of unsuccessful business ventures and unhappily terminated jobs behind him, and only that $400 check from Thomas Newell Metcalf for one of his interplanetary daydreams to show for endless hours spent trying to earn food-money with his pen!

Through the glass paneling the American caught a glimpse of a large and luxurious room, in which a considerable number of men were sitting about and reading papers, each in his own small nook. The American entered a small chamber which looked out into Pall Mall, and for the first time beheld the man whose astonishing revelations would change the life of his guest and to a truly unbelievable degree the culture of the entire western world.

This second man, dressed in the formal evening clothes of the proper Briton, was surprisingly like his guest in physical makeup. Not quite as tall as the American, he was equally stocky in figure, powerfully constructed with the hands of one who had spent years working on the torn or ill bodies of his fellow-man. A thatch of iron-colored hair surmounted his craggy face, which was marked also by steely eyebrows and a moustache of the same metallic tint. As he stepped forward to greet his guest it was obvious that an old wound, long since healed but never forgotten, was stinging him once again.

'Mr. Edgar Rice Burroughs of Chicago,' the gray-haired man said, 'I am so very pleased that you could come. I trust that you have not found our London weather too damp and chilly for one more used to the sunny plains of America. I fear that even an habitual Londoner like myself finds himself reminded of a certain Jezail bullet on a night such as this one.'

The Chicagoan stepped forward to exchange a hearty handshake with his host. 'Chicago in November is hardly a place that I would call the sunny plains, Dr. Watson.' He paused as a humorous rumble emerged from deep in his massive frame. 'But thank you anyway for your thought. This cold wind makes me feel almost at home, but frankly I'm just as happy to be here in your club. I must admit, though, after a glance at the reading room and your club rules here in the Stranger's Room, that it seems like a pretty odd club.'

'The Diogenes Club, to quote an esteemed friend of mine, contains the most unsociable and unclubable men in London,' returned the doctor, a slight Scottish burr becoming audible as he spoke. 'My friend introduced me to the Diogenes Club over twenty years ago. He called it then the queerest club in London, and he was then correct, as he usually is.

112

'But come, Mr. Burroughs, I am forgetting my manners. Will you take off your greatcoat and make yourself comfortable, or would you rather we make our way to a nearby restaurant or to my home. It is a bit out of the way — that is why I suggested our meeting here — but I am certain that Mrs. Watson would not object to an American visitor on so unpleasant a night.'

The big American stirred uncomfortably, still in his damp and heavy outer garment. 'I don't want to seem ungracious, doctor, but as you may know I'm only in London for a few days. It was supposed to be a business deal that didn't work out. The trip alone cost me most of the ready cash I could drum up and I'll be heading for home very soon. Now your telegram mentioned something of interest and possible profit, and if you'll pardon my bluntness, would you please tell me what it is.'

'My dear Mr. Burroughs,' replied Watson, 'I assure you that I am not leading you down any blind path. I perhaps failed to mention that I have of late become addicted to your American pulp magazines through an old interest in sea stories, and have even entered into some correspondence with several editors. One of them, Mr. Metcalf of the Munsey concern, recently sent me a letter describing most enthusiastically a tale of your own authorship, which he promises for the February number. It is he who mentioned that you would shortly be visiting our country.

'In honesty, Mr. Burroughs, I regard myself as a colleague of yours. If you read our British periodicals you may have noticed a number of stories in which I claim the pride of authorship, placed over a period of years by my friend Dr. Doyle with such magazines as *Beeton's* and *The Strand*. I have recently become acquainted with a most remarkable narrative, brought to my attention by the elder brother of my very good friend. Unfortunately, my agent informs me that he cannot place the tale for me; he claims that it is too much like the works of another of his clients, a Mr. Malone, whom he does not wish to offend.

'The story is yours, Mr. Burroughs, if

you would care to place it in America; I would rather not see it in a British magazine, at least in its initial appearance. I fear that neither my agent nor his other client would think that I had any business giving it to you, Mr. Burroughs, or to any other. But I disagree. It is a fantastic and perhaps somewhat lurid tale, but I can vouch for its truth. I ask only that my name not be associated with its publication.'

The American, who had listened intently to his host's offer, held his chin characteristically in one brawny hand. The offer indeed interested him, and promised profit if it came up to Munsey's standards. If not — it would cost him nothing to let the old Scotsman spin a yarn. London was a cold and lonesome city for a visitor who had to count every penny, the Diogenes was warm and comfortable. And, he noticed, a well-stocked bar stood unobtrusively in one corner of the room. Still . . .

'What's in it for you?'

'Eh, I don't understand the idiom, Mr. Burroughs. What's in what?' asked Watson.

'I mean, doctor, what do you get out of giving me this story? A percentage if I sell it? You certainly didn't come down here tonight just to meet me and tell me a tall tale!'

'Very well, Mr. Burroughs. I can see that you have had some unpleasant experiences with life to date.'

'Indeed I have, doctor. I won't try to fool you, I come from a pretty good family in America but things haven't gone so well the past few years. You can tell that. Look at my clothes. I've had to raise my family in some pretty tough neighborhoods. On one occasion my wife had to pawn her wedding ring to put bread on the table.

'I'm not used to getting something for nothing and I don't think I'm getting it now. What's in it for you?' he asked again.

'Ah, I see,' said Watson. 'And that is the very thing that interests me in you. All I want is information about America, particularly your city of Chicago, and most particularly its — did you say — pretty tough neighborhoods.'

'Why?'

'Well,' Watson smiled, 'let us say that I was planning to write a story with its setting in America. I should not like to commit errors in my background. Such information as the schedules of your street railways can be obtained from guidebooks or the *American Almanac*, but authentic information on American, er, American criminal organizations is not readily available.'

'Is that all,' Burroughs laughed, settling back in his easy chair, 'Fair enough. A story for the background for a story. Well, who goes first?'

★ ★ ★

And a story it was indeed! For the story told by John H. Watson is one that the visiting American gave to the world under the title *Tarzan of the Apes*. One may be certain that the beverage service of the Diogenes Club was kept busy that evening. And did Mr. Burroughs honor the plea of Dr. Watson, that the latter's name remain unattached to the tale? He did, and yet he managed to provide sufficient clues in the opening paragraphs of his recounting of the *Fuwalda* tragedy and its fantastic *sequelae* to provide his benefactor, at least, with an assurance that he was remembered, and that the favor was appreciated.

For Burroughs tells us in the opening words of chapter 1, 'Out to Sea,' that 'I had this story from one who had no business to tell it to me, or to any other. I may credit the seductive influence of an old vintage upon the narrator for the beginning of it, and my own skeptical incredulity during the days that followed for the balance of the strange tale.' One sees Burroughs giving back to Watson almost his precise words, and one detects a tongue-in-cheek reminder of the liquid refreshments shared by the two in the Stranger's Room of the Diogenes Club (for one recalls, or at least can find in Watson's 'The Greek Interpreter,' that talking was strictly forbidden elsewhere in the club).

Burroughs also tells us that the story is based upon 'the yellow, mildewed pages of the diary of a man long dead, and the records of the Colonial Office, which dovetail perfectly with the narrative of my convivial host.' And this raises the question of what either Watson or Burroughs was doing examining the unquestionably confidential records of the British Foreign Office.

The answer is obvious. Watson was himself not a member of the Diogenes Club, nor even was his good friend and sometime fellow lodger Sherlock Holmes. No, Watson's access to the Diogenes Club, although directly provided by Sherlock Holmes, was actually dependent upon Sherlock's elder brother Mycroft Holmes. About Mycroft, in Watson's 'The Adventure of the Bruce-Partington Plans,' Sherlock says 'His Pall Mall lodgings, the Diogenes Club, Whitehall — that is his cycle.' Whitehall is of course the home of the British Foreign Office, the equivalent of our own State Department's Foggy Bottom. And again, in the same story, Watson quotes the following conversation between himself and the great sleuth:

* * *

' . . . By the way, do you know what Mycroft is?'

I had some vague recollection of an explanation at the time of the Adventure of the Greek Interpreter.

'You told me that he had some small office under the British government.'

Holmes chuckled.

'I did not know you quite so well in those days. One has to be discreet when one talks of high matters of state. You are right in thinking that he is under the British government. You would also be right in a sense if you said that occasionally he is the British government.'

And yet again, Watson quotes Sherlock concerning Mycroft: 'All other men are specialists, but his specialism is omniscience. We will suppose that a minister needs information as to a point which involves the Navy, India, Canada and the bimetallic question; he could get his separate advices from the various departments upon each, but only Mycroft can focus them all, and say offhand how each factor would affect the other.'

Access to Foreign Office records? For Mycroft, the veriest child's play!

But one wonders why Watson made it a point to lure Burroughs — and one can hardly use any other word than lure — to the Diogenes Club, and why he made such a point of permitting himself to reveal the facts in the case of the barkentine *Fuwalda* as he did. His seeking information about the American underworld seems to be a somewhat farfetched explanation. Watson did, of course, set two of his stories largely in the United States: both *A Study in Scarlet* and *The Valley of Fear* contain lengthy retrospective sections set in America, although neither takes place in Chicago. *A Study in Scarlet* was published twenty-four years before the until-now unrevealed meeting with Burroughs. But *The Valley of Fear* was first published late in 1914, it does contain major sections concerning the American underworld, and the information used by Watson might well have been provided partially or completely by Burroughs.

Still, one seeks some greater motivation

for Watson's actions, and especially so in view of the initially perplexing — but ultimately revealing — complicity of Mycroft Holmes in an incident that must in ordinary circumstances be considered one which would hardly interest the corpulent elder sibling of the great deducer.

For in the Holmes-and-Watson tale 'His Last Bow,' we find the vital clues! One of the few stories in the Canon not written by Watson, this one is attributed by William S. Baring-Gould in his *Sherlock Holmes of Baker Street* to Mycroft himself. In the tale Sherlock Holmes tells Watson of his adventures under the pseudonym of Altamont in demolishing a German spy ring in England, the final capture of the master spy Von Bork taking place in August of 1914. Holmes had long been in retirement practicing bee culture and working at literary projects in a small farm upon the South Downs, and in reply to Watson's question regarding his return to work, he says:

'Ah, I have often marveled at it myself.

The Foreign Minister alone I could have withstood, but when the Premier also deigned to visit my humble roof — !
. . . It has cost me two years, Watson, but they have not been devoid of excitement. When I say that I started my pilgrimage at Chicago, graduated in an Irish secret society at Buffalo, gave serious trouble to the constabulary at Skibbareen, and so eventually caught the eye of a subordinate agent of Von Bork, who recommended me as a likely man, you will realize that the matter was complex.'

How complex it was even 'His Last Bow' does not reveal. Two years culminating in 1914 bring Holmes's pilgrimage, beginning in Chicago, back to 1912. Watson's meeting with Burroughs took place late in 1911. Holmes acted at the entreaty of the Foreign Minister and the Premier; Mycroft on that occasion very likely 'was' the British government. Edgar Rice Burroughs was in London in pursuit of 'a business deal which promptly fell through;' in all likelihood the entire 'deal' was arranged by one Holmes or the other specifically to bring Burroughs to

England. And although the deal 'promptly fell through,' Burroughs' receipt of *Tarzan of the Apes* must be rated as the grandest consolation prize in all the history of literature.

Continuing to examine motives, one notes that Sherlock Holmes was preparing himself for a perilous masquerade beginning in the Chicago underworld. He desperately needed advance information. It is known that Edgar Rice Burroughs knew the Chicago underworld well — one need only examine *The Efficiency Expert* or *The Girl from Farris's* to see as much. And Burroughs was obviously a man capable of keen observation and graphic description. What better source of data! Yet Sherlock was reluctant to question Burroughs personally. Perhaps his motive was an unwillingness to leave his beloved bees any sooner than necessary, or more likely, despite his mastery of the art of disguise, Sherlock did not wish to risk meeting in London a man he might later encounter, in another identity, in America. And so the faithful Watson was called upon once more to enact the role of the unknowing but invaluable cat's-paw.

We know of the success of the bargain. 'A story for the background for a story.' *Tarzan of the Apes* for The *Valley of Fear* . . . and the destruction of the critically dangerous Von Bork spy ring in England three years later.

All of this ratiocination may seem somewhat farfetched to the reader unfamiliar with Holmesian scholarship, and so a further examination of the two Canons involved may, by providing the corroborative evidence which is the second anonymous narrator of *Tarzan of the Apes* as none other than John H. Watson, MD. (For the first anonymous narrator is obviously Edgar Rice Burroughs himself.)

Let us, then, first of all consider the question of Tarzan's identity. As was pointed out both in Pastor Heins's introduction to the first edition of *Edgar Rice Burroughs: Master of Adventure* and in the main text of that volume, Tarzan's 'real' name is not John Clayton at all. In *Tarzan of the Apes* Burroughs refers to 'a certain young Englishman, whom we shall call John Clayton, Lord Greystoke.' This is obviously not his real name, which is never revealed, although we are told that 'Political ambition had caused him to seek transference from the army to the Colonial Office . . . ' . . . and into the province of Mycroft Holmes!

Tarzan of the Apes clearly begins on a bright May morning in 1888, at which time 'Clayton' 'had been married a scarce three months to the Hon. Alice Rutherford.'

Not very long before this occurrence another encounter involving John Clayton had taken place. Sherlockian scholars generally agree on dating this other incident late in September, but do not agree on the year . . . September 26, 1887 seems the most likely date. Watson — who, after all, first gave Burroughs the saga of John Clayton — describes the earlier incident in *The Hound of the Baskervilles*, Chapter 5, 'Three Broken Threads.' To quote a portion of Watson's narration:

The ring at the bell proved to be something even more satisfactory than an answer, however, for the door opened and a rough-looking fellow entered who was evidently the man himself.

'I got a message from the head office that a gent at this address had been inquiring for No. 2704,' said he. 'I've driven straight from the Yard to ask you to your face what you had against me.'

'I have nothing in the world against you, my good man,' said Holmes. 'On the contrary, I have half a sovereign for you if you will give me a clear answer to my questions.'

'Well, I've had a good day and no mistake,' said the cabman with a grin. 'What was it you wanted to ask, sir?'

'First of all your name and address, in case I want you again.'

'John Clayton, 3 Turpey Street, the Borough. My cab is out of Shipley's Yard, near Waterloo Street.'

Notice, then, how cleverly Mycroft presents his agent to Sherlock, providing in the presence of the trusting Watson a complete dossier for Holmes's information, on the undercover agent's assumed identity, appearance, occupation, home and business addresses! What mysterious case the 'young English nobleman' was working on in Behalf of Mycroft — and Whitehall — we do not know. That it was connected with the Baskerville case (which involved Canada and was hence of concern to Mycroft) is possible but by no means certain. At any rate, by the following February 'Clayton' was married; by May he and his bride were aboard the barkentine *Fuwalda*, 'which was to bear them to their final destination.

'And here John, Lord Greystoke, and Lady Alice, his wife, vanished from the eyes and from the knowledge of men.'

Consider now the following reference by Watson in 'The Problem of Thor Bridge,' first published in 1922, long after Burroughs had chronicled the tragedy of the *Fuwalda*: 'No less remarkable is that of the cutter *Alicia*, which sailed one spring morning into a small patch of mist from where she never again emerged, nor was anything further ever heard of herself and her crew.'

A cutter is not exactly the same sort of sailing ship as is a barkentine. The latter, a common reference book states, is 'a three-masted vessel having the fore-mast square-rigged and the others fore- and-aft rigged.' While a cutter, the same volume tells us, is 'a fore-and-aft rigged vessel with one mast and a jib and forestaysail.' Since Watson was quite a fan of nautical fiction while Burroughs was more interested in horsemanship and military matters, it seems likely that the *Fuwalda/Alicia* was indeed a cutter rather than a barkentine. One may surmise that the author of *Tarzan of the Apes* recalled Watson's description of fore-and-aft rigging but strangely forgot the simpler statement of the number of masts on the ship, and called the cutter a barkentine. Watson's later passing reference may well have been a friendly dig in return for Burroughs' reference to 'the seductive influence of an old vintage' upon Watson.

As for the names of the ship in the two stories, one can only wonder whether Watson was deliberately 'coding' the identification, or whether his memory was playing tricks upon the doctor some thirty-two years after the event of the cutter's disappearance and eleven years after Watson had first mentioned the event to Burroughs. At any event, we have the cutter — not barkentine — *Fuwalda*, carrying John, Lord Greystoke, and Lady Alice, his wife . . . transformed into the cutter *Alicia*. The reference is obvious.

And if it was merely a quirk of memory, let us not deride the doctor too unkindly, for as early as 1913 in *The Return of Tarzan*, Edgar Rice Burroughs gave the name of Lord Tennington's ocean-going yacht as the *Lady Alice*. Heaven knows what the real name of that vessel could have been! The *Friesland?*

And so it went, over the years. Burroughs chronicling the saga of Tarzan, Watson recording the adventures of Sherlock Holmes, and the two impinging upon one another only in ways too subtle for the casual observer to detect. There was, of course, the appearance of Tarzan's father in Watson's *Hound of the Baskervilles* and Burroughs' passing reference to Sherlock Holmes in *The Son of Tarzan*. But except for these two namings of names one must learn to observe and

130

deduce, as in the case of the *Fuwalda*, the *Lady Alice*, and the *Alicia*, the visits of Tarzan to England and America over the years, his adoption of formal detection techniques in 'Tarzan and the Jungle Murders,' and other references yet to be brought to light.

One can only wonder whether Burroughs and Watson kept up a correspondence, or ever again exchanged visits. One can wonder whether Sherlock ever made it a point to meet the son of his old acquaintance John Clayton. One may wonder, but I fear that one will never know.

AUTHOR'S NOTE:

The author wishes to acknowledge the assistance and encouragement of such Sherlockian scholars as Vincent Starrett, P. Christian Steinbrunner, Roger Lancelyn Green, David G. Van Arnam, and Professor H. W. Starr, whose, guidance in an unfamiliar Canon has proved indispensable. Special note should be made of Professor Starr's essay in The Baker Street Journal for January, 1960, the first published work on the relationship of two brilliant Canons. Although certain of Professor Starr's conclusions are at variance with those of the present work, his achievement as a pioneer is beyond dispute.

Four

The Adventure of The Voorish Sign

It was by far the most severe winter London had known in human memory, perhaps since the Romans had founded their settlement of Londinium nearly two millennia ago. Storms had swept down from the North Sea, cutting off the Continent and blanketing the great metropolis with thick layers of snow that were quickly blackened by the choking fumes of ten thousand charcoal braziers, turning to a treacherous coating of ice when doused with only slightly warmer peltings of sleet.

Even so, Holmes and I were snug in our quarters at 221B Baker Street. The fire had been laid, we had consumed a splendid dinner of meat pasties and red cabbage served by the ever-reliable Mrs. Hudson, and I found myself dreaming over an aged brandy and a pipe while Holmes devoted himself to his newest passion.

He had raided our slim exchequer for sufficient funds to purchase one of Mr. Emile Berliner's new gramophones, imported by Harrods of Brompton Road. He had placed one of Mr. Berliner's new disk recordings on the machine, advertised as a marked improvement over the traditional wax cylinders. But the sounds that emerged from the horn were neither pleasant nor tuneful to my ears. Instead they were of a weird and disquieting nature, seemingly discordant yet suggestive of strange harmonies which it would be better not to understand.

As I was about to ask Holmes to shut off the contraption, the melody came to an end and Holmes removed the needle from its groove.

Holmes pressed an upraised finger against his thin lips and sharply uttered my name. 'Watson!' he repeated as I lowered my pipe. The brandy snifter had very nearly slipped from my grasp, but I was able to catch it in time to prevent a disastrous spill.

'What is it, Holmes?' I inquired.

'Listen!'

He held one hand aloft, an expression of intense concentration upon his saturnine features. He nodded toward the shuttered windows which gave out upon Baker Street.

'I hear nothing except the whistle of the wind against the eaves,' I told him.

'Listen more closely.'

I tilted my head, straining to hear whatever it was that had caught Holmes's attention. There was a creak from below, followed by the sound of a door opening and closing, and a rapping of knuckles against solid wood, the latter sound muffled as by thin cloth.

I looked at Holmes, who pressed a long finger against his lips, indicating that silence was required. He nodded toward our door, and in a few moments I heard the tread of Mrs. Hudson ascending to our lodging. Her sturdy pace was accompanied by another, light and tentative in nature.

Holmes drew back our front door to reveal our landlady, her hand raised to knock. 'Mr. Holmes!' she gasped.

'Mrs. Hudson, I see that you have brought with you Lady Fairclough of Pontefract. Will you be so kind as to permit Lady Fairclough to enter, and would you be so good as to brew a hot cup of tea for my lady. She must be suffering from her trip through this wintry night.'

Mrs. Hudson turned away and made her way down the staircase while the slim young woman who had accompanied her entered our sitting room with a series of long, graceful strides. Behind her, Mrs. Hudson had carefully placed a carpetbag valise upon the floor.

'Lady Fairclough.' Holmes addressed the newcomer. 'May I introduce my associate, Dr. Watson. Of course you know who I am, which is why you have come to seek my assistance. But first, please warm yourself by the fire. Dr. Watson will fetch a bottle of brandy with which we will fortify the hot tea that Mrs. Hudson is preparing.'

The newcomer had not said a word, but her face gave proof of her astonishment that Holmes had known her identity and home without being told. She wore a stylish hat trimmed in dark fur and a carefully tailored coat with matching decorations at collar and cuffs. Her feet were covered in boots that disappeared beneath the lower hem of her coat.

I helped her off with her outer garment. By the time I had placed it in our closet, Lady Fairclough was comfortably settled in our best chair, holding slim hands toward the cheerily dancing flames. She had removed her gloves and laid them with seemingly careless precision across the wooden arm of her chair.

'Mr. Holmes,' she said in a voice that spoke equally of cultured sensitivity and barely repressed terror, 'I apologize for disturbing you and Dr. Watson at this late hour, but — '

'There is no need for apologies, Lady Fairclough. On the contrary, you are to be commended for having the courage to cross the Atlantic in the midst of winter, and the captain of the steamship *Murania* is to be congratulated for having negotiated the crossing successfully. It is unfortunate that our customs agents delayed your disembarkation as they did, but now that you are here, perhaps you will enlighten Dr. Watson and myself as to the problem which has beset your brother, Mr. Philip Llewellyn.'

If Lady Fairclough had been startled by Holmes's recognizing her without introduction, she was clearly amazed beyond my meager powers of description by this statement. She raised a hand to her cheek, which showed a smoothness of complexion and grace of curve in the flattering glow of the dancing flames. 'Mr. Holmes,' she exclaimed, 'how did you know all that?'

'It was nothing, Lady Fairclough, one need merely keep one's senses on the alert and one's mind active.' A glance that Holmes darted in my direction was not welcome, but I felt constrained from protesting in the presence of a guest and potential client.

'So you say, Mr. Holmes, but I have read of your exploits and in many cases they seem little short of supernatural,' Lady Fairclough replied.

'Not in the least. Let us consider the

present case. Your valise bears the paper label of the Blue Star Line. The *Murania* and the *Lemuria* are the premiere ocean liners of the Blue Star Line, alternating upon the easterly and westerly transatlantic sea-lanes. Even a fleeting glance at the daily shipping news indicates that the *Murania* was due in Liverpool early this morning. If the ship made port at even so late an hour as ten o'clock, in view of the fact that the rail journey from Liverpool to London requires a mere two hours, you should have reached our city by noon. Another hour at most from the rail terminus to Baker Street would have brought you to our door by one o'clock this afternoon. And yet,' concluded Holmes, glancing at the ormolu clock that rested upon our mantel, 'you arrive at the surprising hour of ten o'clock *post meridian*.'

'But, Holmes,' I interjected, 'Lady Fairclough may have had other errands to perform before coming to us.'

'No, Watson, no. I fear that you have failed to draw the proper inference from that which you have surely observed. You did note, did you not, that Lady Fairclough has brought her carpetbag with her?'

I pled guilty to the charge.

'Surely, had she not been acting in great haste, Lady Fairclough would have gone to her hotel, refreshed herself, and left her luggage in her quarters there before traveling to Baker Street. The fact that she has but one piece of luggage with her gives further testimony to the urgency with which she departed her home in Canada. Now, Watson, what could have caused Lady Fairclough to commence her trip in such haste?'

I shook my head. 'I confess that I am at a loss.'

'It was but eight days ago that the *Daily Mail* carried a dispatch marked Merthyr Tydfil, a town situated some miles from the border of England and Wales, concerning the mysterious disappearance of Mr. Philip Llewellyn. There would have been time for word to reach Lady Fairclough in Pontefract by transatlantic cable. Fearing that delay in traveling to the port and boarding the *Murania* would cause intolerable delay, Lady Fairclough had her maid pack the fewest possible necessities in her carpetbag. She then made her way to Halifax, whence the *Murania* departed, and upon reaching Liverpool this morning would have made her way at once to London. Yet she arrived some nine hours later than she might have been expected to do. Since our rail service remains uninterrupted in even the most severe of climatic conditions, it can only have been the customs service, equally notorious for their punctilio and their dilatory conduct, which could be responsible.'

Turning once more to Lady Fairclough, Holmes said, 'In behalf of Her Majesty's Customs Service, Lady Fairclough, I tender my apologies.'

There was a knock at the door and Mrs. Hudson appeared, bearing a tray with hot tea and cold sandwiches. This she placed upon the table, then took her leave.

Lady Fairclough looked at the repast and said, 'Oh, I simply could not.'

'Nonsense,' Holmes insisted. 'You have completed an arduous journey and face a dangerous undertaking. You must keep up your strength.' He rose and added brandy to Lady Fairclough's tea, then stood commandingly over her while she consumed the beverage and two sandwiches.

'I suppose I was hungry after all,' she admitted at last. I was pleased to see some color returning to her cheeks. I had been seriously concerned about her wellbeing.

'Now, Lady Fairclough,' said Holmes, 'it might be well for you to go to your hotel and restore your strength with a good night's slumber. You do have a reservation, I trust.'

'Oh, of course, at Claridge's. A suite was ordered for me through the courtesy of the Blue Star Line, but I could not rest now, Mr. Holmes. I am far too distraught to sleep until I have explained my need to you, and received your assurance that you and Dr. Watson will take my case. I have plenty of money, if that is a concern.'

Holmes indicated that financial details could wait, but I was pleased to be included in our guest's expression of need. So often I find myself taken for granted, while in fact I am Holmes's trusted associate, as he has himself acknowledged on many occasions.

'Very well.' Holmes nodded, seating himself opposite Lady Fairclough. 'Please tell me your story in your own words, being as precise with details as possible.'

Lady Fairclough drained her cup and waited while Holmes filled it once again with brandy and a spot of Darjeeling. She downed another substantial draft, then launched upon her narrative.

'As you know, Mr. Holmes — and Dr. Watson — I was born in England of old stock. Despite our ancient Welsh connections and family name, we have been English for a thousand years. I was the elder of two children, the younger being my brother, Philip. As a daughter, I saw little future for myself in the home islands, and accepted the proposal of marriage tendered by my husband, Lord Fairclough, whose Canadian holdings are substantial and who indicated to me a desire to emigrate to Canada and build a new life there, which we would share.'

I had taken out my notebook and

fountain pen and begun jotting notes.

'At about this time my parents were both killed in a horrendous accident, the collision of two trains in the Swiss Alps while vacationing abroad. Feeling that an elaborate wedding would be disrespectful of the deceased, Lord Fairclough and I were quietly married and took our leave of England. We lived happily in Pontefract, Canada, until my husband disappeared.'

'Indeed,' Holmes interjected, 'I had read of Lord Fairclough's disappearance. I note that you refer to him as your husband rather than your late husband still, nor do I see any mourning band upon your garment. Is it your belief that your husband lives still?'

Lady Fairclough lowered her eyes for a moment as a flush rose to her cheeks. 'Although ours was somewhat a marriage of convenience, I find that I have come to love my husband most dearly. There was no discord between us, if you are concerned over such, Mr. Holmes.'

'Not in the least, Lady Fairclough.'

'Thank you.' She sipped from her teacup. Holmes peered at it, then refreshed its contents once again. 'Thank you,' Lady Fairclough repeated. 'My husband had been corresponding with his brother-in-law, my brother, and later, after my brother's marriage, with my brother's wife, for some time before he disappeared. I saw the envelopes as they came and went, but I was never permitted to so much as lay eyes on their contents. After reading each newly delivered letter, my husband would burn it and crush the ashes beyond recovery. After receiving one very lengthy letter — I could tell it was lengthy by the heft of the envelope in which it arrived — my husband summoned carpenters and prepared a sealed room which I was forbidden to enter. Of course I obeyed my husband's command.'

'A wise policy,' I put in. 'One knows the story of Bluebeard.'

'He would lock himself in his private chamber for hours at a time, sometimes days. When he disappeared, in fact, I half expected him to return at any moment.' Lady Fairclough put her hand to her throat. 'Please,' she said softly, 'I beg your pardon for the impropriety, but I feel suddenly so warm.' I glanced away, and when I looked back at her I observed that the top button of her blouse had been undone.

'My husband has been gone now for two years, and all have given him up for dead save myself, and I will concede that even my hopes are of the faintest. During the period of correspondence between my husband and my brother, my husband began to absent himself from all human society from time to time. Gradually the frequency and duration of his disappearances increased. I feared I knew not what — perhaps that he had become addicted to some drug or unspeakable vice for the indulging of which he preferred isolation. I inferred that he had caused the construction of the sealed room for this purpose, and determined that I should learn its secret.'

She bowed her head and drew a series of long, sobbing breaths, which caused her graceful bosom visibly to heave. After a time she raised her face. Her cheeks were wet with tears. She resumed her narrative.

'I summoned a locksmith from the village and persuaded him to aid me in gaining entry. When I stood at last in my husband's secret chamber I found myself confronting a room completely devoid of feature. The ceiling, the walls, the floor were all plain and devoid of ornament. There were neither windows nor fireplace, nor any other means of egress from the room.'

Holmes nodded, frowning. 'There was nothing noteworthy about the room, then?' he asked at length.

'Yes, Mr. Holmes, there was.' Lady Fairclough's response startled me so, I nearly dropped my fountain pen, but I recovered and returned to my note taking.

'At first the room seemed a perfect cube. The ceiling, floor, and four walls each appeared absolutely square and mounted at a precise right angle to one another. But as I stood there, they seemed to — I suppose, *shift* is the closest

I can come to it, Mr. Holmes, but they did not actually move in any familiar manner. And yet their shape seemed to be different, and the angles to become peculiar, obtuse, and to open onto other — how to put this? — *dimensions*.'

She seized Holmes's wrist in her graceful fingers and leaned toward him pleadingly. 'Do you think I am insane, Mr. Holmes? Has my grief driven me to the brink of madness? There are times when I think I can bear no more strangeness.'

'You are assuredly not insane,' Holmes told her. 'You have stumbled upon one of the strangest and most dangerous of phenomena, a phenomenon barely suspected by even the most advanced of mathematical theoreticians and spoken of even by them in only the most cautious of whispers.'

He withdrew his arm from her grasp, shook his head, and said, 'If your strength permits, you must continue your story, please.'

'I will try,' she answered.

I waited, fountain pen poised above notebook.

Our visitor shuddered as with a fearsome recollection. 'Once I had left the secret room, sealing it behind myself, I attempted to resume a normal life. It was days later that my husband reappeared, refusing as usual to give any explanation of his recent whereabouts. Shortly after this a dear friend of mine living in Quebec gave birth to a child. I had gone to be with her when word was received of the great Pontefract earthquake. In this disaster a fissure appeared in the earth and our house was completely swallowed. I was, fortunately, left in a state of financial independence, and have never suffered from material deprivation. But I have never again seen my husband. Most believe that he was in the house at the time of its disappearance, and was killed at once, but I retain a hope, however faint, that he may somehow have survived.'

She paused to compose herself, then resumed.

'But I fear I am getting ahead of myself. It was shortly before my husband ordered the construction of his sealed room that my brother, Philip, announced his engagement and the date of his impending nuptials. I thought the shortness of his intended period of engagement was unseemly, but in view of my own marriage and departure to Canada so soon after my parents' death, I was in no position to condemn Philip. My husband and I booked passage to England, on the *Lemuria* in fact, and from Liverpool made our way to the family lands in Merthyr Tydfil.'

She shook her head as if to free it of an unpleasant memory.

'Upon arriving at Anthracite Palace, I was shocked by my brother's appearance.'

At this point I interrupted our guest with a query.

'Anthracite Palace? Is that not an unusual name for a family manse?'

'Our family residence was so named by my ancestor, Sir Llewys Llewellyn, who built the family fortune, and the manor, by operating a network of successful coal mines. As you are probably aware, the region is rich in anthracite. The Llewellyns pioneered modern mining methods which rely upon gelignite explosives to loosen banks of coal for the miners to remove from their native sites. In the region of Merthyr Tydfil, where the Anthracite Palace is located, the booming of gelignite charges is heard to this day, and stores of the explosive are kept at the mine heads.'

I thanked her for the clarification and suggested that she continue with her narrative.

'My brother was neatly barbered and clothed, but his hands shook, his cheeks were sunken, and his eyes had a frightened, hunted look to them,' she said. 'When I toured my childhood home I was shocked to find its interior architecture modified. There was now a sealed room, just as there had been at Pontefract. I was not permitted to enter that room. I expressed my concern at my brother's appearance but he insisted he was well and introduced his fiancée, who was already living at the palace.'

I drew my breath with a gasp.

'Yes, Doctor,' Lady Fairclough responded, 'you heard me correctly. She was a woman of dark, Gypsyish complexion, glossy sable

153

hair, and darting eyes. I disliked her at once. She gave her own name, not waiting for Philip to introduce her properly. Her maiden name, she announced, was Anastasia Romelly. She claimed to be of noble Hungarian blood, allied both to the Hapsburgs and the Romanovs.'

'Humph,' I grunted, 'Eastern European nobility is a ha'penny a dozen, and three-quarters of them aren't real even at that.'

'Perhaps true,' Holmes snapped at me, 'but we do not know that the credentials of the lady involved were other than authentic.' He frowned and turned away. 'Lady Fairclough, please continue.'

'She insisted on wearing her native costume. And she had persuaded my brother to replace his chef with one of her own choosing, whom she had imported from her homeland and who replaced our usual menu of good English fare with unfamiliar dishes reeking of odd spices and unknown ingredients. She imported strange wines and ordered them served with meals.'

I shook my head in disbelief.

'The final straw came upon the day of her wedding to my brother. She insisted upon being given away by a surly, dark man who appeared for the occasion, performed his duty, and then disappeared. She — '

'A moment, please,' Holmes interrupted. 'If you will forgive me — you say that this man disappeared. Do you mean that he took his leave prematurely?'

'No, I do not mean that at all.' Lady Fairclough was clearly excited. A moment earlier she had seemed on the verge of tears. Now she was angry and eager to unburden herself of her tale.

'In a touching moment, he placed the bride's hand upon that of the groom. Then he raised his own hand. I thought his intent was to place his benediction upon the couple, but such was not the case. He made a gesture with his hand, as if making a mystical sign.'

She raised her own hand from her lap, but Holmes snapped, 'Do not, I warn you, attempt to replicate the gesture! Please, if you can, simply describe it to Dr. Watson and myself.'

'I could not replicate the gesture if I tried,' Lady Fairclough said. 'It defies imitation. I cannot even describe it accurately, I fear. I was fascinated and tried to follow the movement of the dark man's fingers, but I could not. They seemed to disappear and reappear most shockingly, and then, without further warning, he was simply gone. I tell you, Mr. Holmes, one moment the dark man was there, and then he was gone.'

'Did no one else take note of this, my lady?'

'No one did, apparently. Perhaps all eyes were trained upon the bride and groom, although I believe I did notice the presiding official exchanging several glances with the dark man. Of course, that was before his disappearance.'

Holmes stroked his jaw, deep in thought. There was a lengthy silence in the room, broken only by the ticking of the ormolu clock and whistling of the wind through the eaves. Finally Holmes spoke.

'It can be nothing other than the Voorish Sign,' he said.

'The Voorish Sign?' Lady Fairclough

repeated inquiringly.

Holmes said, 'Never mind. This becomes more interesting by the moment, and also more dangerous. Another question, if you please. Who was the presiding official at the wedding? He was, I would assume, a priest of the Church of England.'

'No.' Lady Fairclough shook her head once again. 'The official was neither a member of the Anglican clergy nor a *he*. The wedding was performed by a woman.'

I gasped in surprise, drawing still another sharp glance from Holmes.

'She wore robes such as I have never seen,' our guest resumed. 'There were symbols, both astronomical and astrological, embroidered in silver thread and gold, green, blue, and red. There were other symbols totally unfamiliar to me, suggestive of strange geometries and odd shapes. The ceremony itself was conducted in a language I had never before heard, and I am something of a linguist, Mr. Holmes. I believe I detected a few words of Old Temple Egyptian, a phrase in Coptic Greek, and several suggestions

157

of Sanskrit. Other words I did not recognize at all.'

Holmes nodded. I could see the excitement growing in his eyes, the excitement that I saw only when a fascinating challenge was presented to him.

He asked, 'What was this person's name?'

'Her name,' Lady Fairclough voiced through teeth clenched in anger, or perhaps in the effort to prevent their chattering with fear, 'was Vladimira Petrovna Ludmilla Romanova. She claimed the title of Archbishop of the Wisdom Temple of the Dark Heavens.'

'Why — why,' I exclaimed, 'I've never heard of such a thing! This is sheer blasphemy!'

'It is something far worse than blasphemy, Watson.' Holmes leaped to his feet and paced rapidly back and forth. At one point he halted near our front window, being careful not to expose himself to the direct sight of anyone lurking below. He peered down into Baker Street, something I have seen him do many times in our years together. Then he did something I had not seen before. Drawing himself back still farther, he gazed upward. What he hoped to perceive in the darkened winter sky other than falling snowflakes, I could hardly imagine.

'Lady Fairclough,' he intoned at length, 'you have been remarkably strong and courageous in your performance here this night. I will now ask Dr. Watson to see you to your hotel. You mentioned Claridge's, I believe. I will ask Dr. Watson to remain in your suite throughout the remainder of the night. I assure you, Lady Fairclough, that he is a person of impeccable character, and your virtue will in no way be compromised by his presence.'

'Even so, Holmes,' I objected, 'the lady's virtue is one thing, her reputation is another.'

The matter was resolved by Lady Fairclough herself. 'Doctor, while I appreciate your concern, we are dealing with a most serious matter. I will accept the suspicious glances of prudes and the smirks of servants if I must. The lives of my husband and my brother are at stake.'

Unable to resist the lady's argument, I followed Holmes's directions and accompanied her to Claridge's. At his insistence I even went so far as to arm myself with a large revolver, which I tucked into the top of my woolen trousers. Holmes warned me, also, to permit no one save himself entry to Lady Fairclough's suite.

Once my temporary charge had retired, I sat in a straight chair, prepared to pass the night in a game of solitaire. Lady Fairclough had donned camisole and hair net and climbed into her bed. I will admit that my cheeks burned, but I reminded myself that in my medical capacity I was accustomed to viewing patients in a disrobed condition, and could surely assume an avuncular role while keeping watch over this courageous lady.

There was a loud rapping at the door. I jerked awake, realizing to my chagrin that I had fallen asleep over my solitary card game. I rose to my feet, went to Lady Fairclough's bedside and assured myself that she was unharmed, and then placed myself at the door to her suite. In response to my demand that our visitor identify himself, a male voice announced simply, 'Room service, guv'ner.'

My hand was on the doorknob, my other hand on the latch, when I remembered Holmes's warning at Baker Street to permit no one entry. Surely a hearty breakfast would be welcome; I could almost taste the kippers and the toast and jam that Mrs. Hudson would have served us, had we been still in our home. But Holmes had been emphatic. What to do? What to do?

'We did not order breakfast.' I spoke through the heavy oaken door.

'Courtesy of the management, guv.'

Perhaps, I thought, I might admit a waiter bearing food. What harm could there be in that? I reached for the latch only to find my hand tugged away by another, that of Lady Fairclough. She had climbed from her bed and crossed the room, barefoot and clad only in her sleeping garment. She shook her head vigorously, drawing me away from the door, which remained latched against any entry. She pointed to me, pantomiming speech. Her message was clear.

'Leave our breakfast in the hall,' I instructed the waiter. 'We shall fetch it in ourselves shortly. We are not ready as yet.'

'Can't do it, sir,' the waiter insisted. 'Please, sir, don't get me in trouble wif the management, guv'ner. I needs to roll my cart into your room and leave the tray. I'll get in trouble if I don't, guv'ner.'

I was nearly persuaded by his plea, but Lady Fairclough had placed herself between me and the door, her arms crossed and a determined expression on her face. Once again she indicated that I should send the waiter away.

'I'm sorry, my man, but I must insist. Simply leave the tray outside our door. That is my final word.'

The waiter said nothing more, but I thought I could hear his reluctantly retreating footsteps.

I retired to make my morning ablutions while Lady Fairclough dressed.

Shortly thereafter, there was another rapping at the door. Fearing the worst, I drew my revolver. Perhaps this was more than a misdirected order for room service. 'I told you to go away,' I commanded.

'Watson, old man, open up. It is I, Holmes.'

The voice was unmistakable; I felt as though a weight of a hundred stone had been lifted from my shoulders. I undid the door latch and stood aside as the best and wisest man I have ever known entered the apartment. I peered out into the hall after he had passed through the doorway. There was no sign of a service cart or breakfast tray.

Holmes asked, 'What are you looking for, Watson?'

I explained the incident of the room-service call.

'You did well, Watson,' he congratulated me. 'You may be certain that was no waiter, nor was his mission one of service to Lady Fairclough and yourself. I have spent the night consulting my files and certain other sources with regard to the odd institution known as the Wisdom Temple of the Dark Heavens, and I can tell you that we are sailing dangerous waters indeed.'

He turned to Lady Fairclough. 'You will please accompany Dr. Watson and myself to Merthyr Tydfil. We shall leave at once. There is a chance that we may yet save the life of your brother, but we have no time to waste.'

Without hesitation, Lady Fairclough strode to the wardrobe, pinned her hat to her hair, and donned the same warm coat she had worn when first I laid eyes on her, mere hours before.

'But, Holmes,' I protested, 'Lady Fairclough and I have not broken our fast.'

'Never mind your stomach, Watson. There is no time to lose. We can purchase sandwiches from a vendor at the station.'

Almost sooner than I can tell, we were seated in a first-class compartment heading westward toward Wales. As good as his word, Holmes had seen to it that we were nourished, and I for one felt the better for having downed even a light and informal meal.

The storm had at last abated and a bright sun shone down from a sky of the most brilliant blue upon fields and hillsides covered with a spotless layer of purest white. Hardly could one doubt the benevolence of the universe; I felt almost like a schoolboy setting off on holiday, but Lady Fairclough's fears and Holmes's serious demeanor brought my soaring spirits back to earth.

'It is as I feared, Lady Fairclough,' Holmes explained. 'Both your brother and your husband have been ensnared in a wicked cult that threatens civilization itself if it is not stopped.'

'A cult?' Lady Fairclough echoed.

'Indeed. You told me that Bishop Romanova was a representative of the Wisdom Temple of the Dark Heavens, did you not?'

'She so identified herself, Mr. Holmes.'

'Yes. Nor would she have reason to lie, not that any denizen of this foul nest would hesitate to do so, should it aid their schemes. The Wisdom Temple is a little-known organization — I would hesitate to dignify them with the title religion — of ancient origins. They have maintained a secretive stance while awaiting some cosmic cataclysm which I fear is nearly upon us.'

'Cosmic — cosmic cataclysm? I say, Holmes, isn't that a trifle melodramatic?' I asked.

'Indeed it is, Watson. But it is nonetheless so. They refer to a coming time 'when the stars are right.' Once that moment arrives, they intend to perform an unholy rite that will 'open the portal,' whatever that means, to admit their masters to the earth. The members of the Wisdom Temple will then become over-seers and oppressors of all humankind, in the service of the dread masters whom they will have admitted to our world.'

I shook my head in disbelief. Outside the windows of our compartment I could see that our train was approaching the trestle that would carry us across the River Severn. It would not be much longer before we should detrain at Merthyr Tydfil.

'Holmes,' I said, 'I would never doubt your word.'

'I know that, old man,' he replied. 'But something is bothering you. Out with it!'

'Holmes, this is madness. Dread masters, opening portals, unholy rites — this is something out of the pages of a penny dreadful. Surely you don't expect Lady Fairclough and myself to believe all this.'

'But I do, Watson. You must believe it, for it is all true, and deadly serious. Lady Fairclough — you have set out to save your brother and if possible your husband, but in fact you have set us in play in a game whose stakes are not one or two mere individuals, but the fate of our planet.'

Lady Fairclough pulled a handkerchief from her wrist and dabbed at her eyes. 'Mr. Holmes, I have seen that strange room at Llewellyn Hall at Pontefract, and I can believe your every word, for all that I agree with Dr. Watson as to the fantastic nature of what you say. Might I ask how you know of this?'

'Very well,' Holmes assented, 'You are entitled to that information. I told you before we left Claridge's that I had spent the night in research. There are many books in my library, most of which are open to my associate, Dr. Watson, and to other men of goodwill, as surely he is. But there are others which I keep under lock and key.'

'I am aware of that, Holmes,' I interjected, 'and I will admit that I have been hurt by your unwillingness to share those volumes with me. Often have I wondered what they contain.'

'Good Watson, it was for your own protection, I assure you. Watson, Lady Fairclough, those books include *De los mundos amenazantes y sombriosos* of Carlos Alfredo de Torrijos, *Emorragia sante* of Luigi Humberto Rosso, and *Das Bestrafen von der Tugendhaft* of Heinrich Ludvig Georg von Feldenstein, as well as the works of the brilliant Mr. Arthur Machen, of whom you may have heard. These tomes, some of them well over a thousand years old and citing still more remote sources whose origins are lost in the mists of antiquity, are frighteningly consistent in their predictions. Further, several of them, Lady Fairclough, refer to a certain powerful and fearsome mystical gesture.'

Although Holmes was addressing our feminine companion, I said, 'Gesture, Holmes? Mystical gesture? What nonsense is this?'

'Not nonsense at all, Watson. You are doubtless aware of the movement that our

Romish brethren refer to as 'crossing themselves.' The Hebrews have a gesture of cabalistic origin that is alleged to bring good luck, and the Gypsies make a sign to turn away the evil eye. Several Asian races perform 'hand dances,' ceremonials of religious or magical significance, including the famous *hoo-la* known on the islands of Oahu and Maui in the Havai'ian archipelago.'

'But these are all foolish superstitions, remnants of an earlier and more credulous age. Surely there is nothing to them, Holmes!'

'I wish I could have your assuredness, Watson. You are a man of science, for which I commend you, but 'There are more things in heaven and earth, Horatio, than are dreamed of in your philosophy.' Do not be too quick, Watson, to dismiss old beliefs. More often than not they have a basis in fact.'

I shook my head and turned my eyes once more to the wintry countryside through which our conveyance was passing. Holmes addressed himself to our companion.

'Lady Fairclough, you mentioned a peculiar gesture that the dark stranger made at the conclusion of your brother's wedding ceremony.'

'I did, yes. It was so strange, I felt almost as if I were being drawn into another world when he moved his hand. I tried to follow the movements, but I could not. And then he was gone.'

Holmes nodded rapidly.

'The Voorish Sign, Lady Fairclough. The stranger was making the Voorish Sign. It is referred to in the works of Machen and others. It is a very powerful and a very evil gesture. You were fortunate that you were not drawn into that other world, fortunate indeed.'

Before much longer we reached the rail terminus nearest to Merthyr Tydfil. We left our compartment and shortly were ensconced in a creaking trap whose driver whipped up his team and headed for the Anthracite Palace. It was obvious from his demeanor that the manor was a familiar landmark in the region.

'We should be greeted by Mrs. Morrissey, our housekeeper, when we reach the manor,' Lady Fairclough said. 'It was she who notified me of my brother's straits. She is the last of our old family retainers to remain with the Llewellyns of Merthyr Tydfil. One by one the new lady of the manor has arranged their departure and replaced them with a swarthy crew of her own countrymen. Oh, Mr. Holmes, it is all so horrid!'

Holmes did his best to comfort the frightened woman.

Soon the Anthracite Palace hove into view. As its name would suggest, it was built of the local native coal. Architects and masons had carved the jet-black deposits into building blocks and created an edifice that stood like a black jewel against the white backing of snow, its battlements glittering in the wintry sunlight.

Our trap was met by a liveried servant who instructed lesser servants to carry our meager luggage into the manor. Lady Fairclough, Holmes, and I were ourselves conducted into the main hall.

The building was lit with oversized candles whose flames were so shielded as to prevent any danger of the coal walls catching fire. It struck me that the Anthracite Palace was one of the strangest architectural conceits I had ever encountered. 'Not a place I would like to live in, eh, Holmes?' I was trying for a tone of levity, but must confess that I failed to achieve it.

We were left waiting for an excessive period of time, in my opinion, but at length a tall wooden door swung back and a woman of commanding presence, exotic in appearance with her swarthy complexion, flashing eyes, sable locks and shockingly reddened lips, entered the hall. She nodded to Holmes and myself and exchanged a frigid semblance of a kiss with Lady Fairclough, whom she addressed as 'sister.'

Lady Fairclough demanded to see her brother, but Mrs. Llewellyn refused conversation until we were shown to our rooms and had time to refresh ourselves. We were summoned, in due course, to the dining hall. I was famished, and both relieved and my appetite further excited by the delicious odors that came to us as we were seated at the long, linen-covered table.

Only four persons were present. These were, of course, Holmes and myself, Lady Fairclough, and our hostess, Mrs. Llewellyn.

Lady Fairclough attempted once again to inquire as to the whereabouts of her brother, Philip.

Her sister-in-law replied only, 'He is pursuing his devotions. We shall see him when the time comes 'round.'

Failing to learn more about her brother, Lady Fairclough asked after the housekeeper, Mrs. Morrissey.

'I have sad news, sister dear,' Mrs. Llewellyn said. 'Mrs. Morrissey was taken ill very suddenly. Philip personally drove into Merthyr Tydfil to fetch a physician for her, but by the time they arrived, Mrs. Morrissey had expired. She was buried in the town cemetery. This all happened just last week. I knew that you were already en route from Canada, and it seemed best not to further distress you with this information.'

'Oh no,' Lady Fairclough gasped. 'Not Mrs. Morrissey! She was like a mother to me. She was the kindest, dearest of women. She — ' Lady Fairclough stopped, pressing her hand to her mouth. She inhaled deeply. 'Very well, then.' I could see a look of determination rising like a banked flame deep in her eye. 'If she has died there is naught to be done for it.'

There was a pillar of strength hidden within this seemingly weak female. I would not care to make an enemy of Lady Fairclough. I noted also that Mrs. Llewellyn spoke English fluently but with an accent that I found thoroughly unpleasant. It seemed to me that she, in turn, found the language distasteful. Clearly, these two were fated to clash. But the tension of the moment was broken by the arrival of our viands.

The repast was sumptuous in appearance, but every course, it seemed to me, had some flaw — an excessive use of spice, an overdone vegetable, an undercooked piece of meat or game, a fish that might have been kept a day too long before serving, a cream that had stood in a warm kitchen an hour longer than was wise. By the end of the meal my appetite had departed, but it was replaced by a sensation of queasiness and discomfort rather than satisfaction.

Servants brought cigars for Holmes and myself, an after-dinner brandy for the men, and sweet sherry for the women, but I put out my cigar after a single draft and noticed that Holmes did the same with his own. Even the beverage seemed in some subtle way to be faulty.

'Mrs. Llewellyn.' Lady Fairclough addressed her sister-in-law when at last the latter seemed unable longer to delay confrontation. 'I received a telegram via transatlantic cable concerning the disappearance of my brother. He failed to greet us upon our arrival, nor has there been any sign of his presence since then. I demand to know his whereabouts.'

'Sister dear,' replied Anastasia Romelly Llewellyn, 'that telegram should never have been sent. Mrs. Morrissey transmitted it from Merthyr Tydfil while in town on an errand for the palace. When I learned of her presumption I determined to send her packing, I can assure you. It was only her unfortunate demise that prevented my doing so.'

At this point my friend Holmes addressed our hostess.

'Madam, Lady Fairclough has journeyed from Canada to learn of her brother's circumstances. She has engaged me, along with my associate, Dr. Watson, to assist her in this enterprise. It is not my desire to make this affair any more unpleasant than is necessary, but I must insist upon your providing the information that Lady Fairclough is seeking.'

I believe at this point that I observed a smirk, or at least the suggestion of one, pass across the face of Mrs. Llewellyn. But she quickly responded to Holmes's demand, her peculiar accent as pronounced and unpleasant as ever.

'We have planned a small religious service for this evening. You are all invited to attend, of course, even though I had expected only my dear sister-in-law to do so. However, the larger group will be accommodated.'

'What is the nature of this religious service?' Lady Fairclough demanded.

Mrs. Llewellyn smiled. 'It will be that of the Wisdom Temple, of course. The

Wisdom Temple of the Dark Heavens. It is my hope that Bishop Romanova herself will preside, but absent her participation we can still conduct the service ourselves.'

I reached for my pocket watch. 'It's getting late, madam. Might I suggest that we get started, then!'

Mrs. Llewellyn turned her eyes upon me. In the flickering candlelight they seemed larger and darker than ever. 'You do not understand, Dr. Watson. It is too early rather than too late to start our ceremony. We will proceed precisely at midnight. Until then, please feel free to enjoy the paintings and tapestries with which the Anthracite Palace is decorated, or pass the time in Mr. Llewellyn's library. Or, if you prefer, you may of course retire to your quarters and seek sleep.'

Thus it was that we three separated temporarily, Lady Fairclough to pass some hours with her husband's chosen books, Holmes to an examination of the palace's art treasures, and I to bed.

I was awakened from a troubled slumber haunted by strange beings of nebulous form. Standing over my bed, shaking me by the shoulder, was my friend Sherlock Holmes. I could see a rim of snow adhering to the edges of his boots.

'Come, Watson,' said he, 'the game is truly afoot, and it is by far the strangest game we are ever likely to pursue.'

Swiftly donning my attire, I accompanied Holmes as we made our way to Lady Fairclough's chamber. She had retired there after spending the hours since dinner in her brother's library, to refresh herself. She must have been awaiting our arrival, for she responded without delay to Holmes's knock and the sound of his voice.

Before we proceeded further Holmes drew me aside. He reached inside his vest and withdrew a small object, which he held concealed in his hand. I could not see its shape, for he held it inside a clenched fist, but I could tell that it emitted a dark radiance, a faint suggestion of which I could see between his fingers.

'Watson,' quoth he, 'I am going to give you this. You must swear to me that you will not look at it, on pain of damage beyond anything you can so much as imagine. You must keep it upon your person, if possible in direct contact with your body, at all times. If all goes well this night, I will ask you to return it to me. If all does not go well, it may save your life.'

I held my hand out towards him.

Placing the object on my outstretched palm, Holmes closed my own fingers carefully around it. Surely this was the strangest object I had ever encountered. It was unpleasantly warm, its texture like that of an overcooked egg, and it seemed to squirm as if it were alive, or perhaps as if it contained something that lived and strove to escape an imprisoning integument.

'Do not look at it,' Holmes repeated. 'Keep it with you at all times. Promise me you will do these things, Watson!'

I assured him that I would do as he requested.

Momentarily we beheld Mrs. Llewellyn moving down the hallway toward us. Her stride was so smooth and her progress so steady that she seemed to be gliding rather than walking. She carried a kerosene lamp whose flame reflected from the polished blackness of the walls, casting ghostly shadows of us all.

Speaking not a word, she gestured to us, summoning us to follow her. We proceeded along a series of corridors and up and down staircases until, I warrant, I lost all sense of direction and of elevation. I could not tell whether we had climbed to a room in one of the battlements of the Anthracite Palace or descended to a dungeon beneath the Llewellyns' ancestral home. I had placed the object Holmes had entrusted to me inside my garments. I could feel it struggling to escape, but it was bound in place and could not do so.

'Where is this bishop you promised us?' I asked of Mrs. Llewellyn.

Our hostess turned toward me. She had replaced her colorful Gypsyish attire with a robe of dark purple. Its color reminded me of the emanations of the warm object concealed now within my own clothing. Her robe was marked with embroidery of a pattern that confused the eye so that I was unable to discern its nature.

'You misunderstood me, Doctor,' she intoned in her unpleasant accent. 'I stated merely that it was my hope that Bishop Romanova would preside at our service. Such is still the case. We shall see in due time.'

We stood now before a heavy door bound with rough iron bands. Mrs. Llewellyn lifted a key which hung suspended about her neck on a ribbon of crimson hue. She inserted it into the lock and turned it. She then requested Holmes and myself to apply our combined strength to opening the door. As we did so, pressing our shoulders against it, my impression was that the resistance came from some willful reluctance rather than a mere matter of weight or decay.

No light preceded us into the room, but Mrs. Llewellyn strode through the doorway carrying her kerosene lamp before her. Its rays now reflected off the walls of the chamber. The room was as Lady Fairclough had described the sealed room in her erstwhile home at Pontefract. The configuration and even the number of surfaces that surrounded us seemed unstable. I was unable even to count them. The very angles at which they met defied my every attempt to comprehend.

An altar of polished anthracite was the sole furnishing of this hideous, irrational chamber.

Mrs. Llewellyn placed her kerosene lamp upon the altar. She turned then, and indicated with a peculiar gesture of her hand that we were to kneel as if participants in a more conventional religious ceremony.

I was reluctant to comply with her silent command, but Holmes nodded to me, indicating that he wished me to do so. I lowered myself, noting that Lady Fairclough and Holmes himself emulated my act.

Before us, and facing the black altar, Mrs. Llewellyn also knelt. She raised her face as if seeking supernatural guidance from above, causing me to remember that the full name of her peculiar sect was the Wisdom Temple of the Dark Heavens. She commenced a weird chanting in a language such as I had never heard, not in all my travels. There was a suggestion of the argot of the dervishes of Afghanistan, something of the Buddhist monks of Tibet, and a hint of the remnant of the ancient Incan language still spoken by the remotest tribes of the high Choco plain of the Chilean Andes, but in fact the language was none of these and the few words that I was able to make out proved both puzzling and suggestive but never specific in their meaning.

As Mrs. Llewellyn continued her chanting, she slowly raised first one hand then the other above her head. Her fingers were moving in an intricate pattern. I tried to follow their progress but found my consciousness fading into a state of confusion. I could have sworn that her fingers twined and knotted like the tentacles of a jellyfish. Their colors, too, shifted: vermilion, scarlet, obsidian. They seemed, even, to disappear into and return from some concealed realm invisible to my fascinated eyes.

The object that Holmes had given me throbbed and squirmed against my body, its unpleasantly hot and squamous presence making me wish desperately to rid myself of it. It was only my pledge to Holmes that prevented me from doing so.

I clenched my teeth and squeezed my eyes shut, summoning up images from my youth and of my travels, holding my hand clasped over the object as I did so. Suddenly the tension was released. The object was still there, but as if it had a consciousness of its own, it seemed to grow calm. My own jaw relaxed and I opened my eyes to behold a surprising sight.

Before me there emerged another figure. As Mrs. Llewellyn was stocky and swarthy, of the model of Gypsy women, this person was tall and graceful. Swathed entirely in jet, with hair a seeming midnight blue and complexion as black as the darkest African, she defied my conventional ideas of beauty with a weird and exotic glamour of her own that defies description. Her features were as finely cut as those of the ancient Ethiopians are said to have been, her movements filled with a grace that would shame the pride of Covent Garden or the Bolshoi.

But whence had this apparition made her way? Still kneeling upon the ebon floor of the sealed room, I shook my head. She seemed to have emerged from the very angle between the walls.

She floated toward the altar, lifted the chimney from the kerosene lamp, and doused its flame with the palm of her bare hand.

Instantly the room was plunged into stygian darkness, but gradually a new light, if so I may describe it, replaced the flickering illumination of the kerosene lamp. It was a light of darkness, if you will, a glow of blackness deeper than the blackness which surrounded us, and yet by its light I could see my companions and my surroundings.

The tall woman smiled in benediction upon the four of us assembled, and gestured toward the angle between the walls. With infinite grace and seemingly glacial slowness she drifted toward the opening, through which I now perceived forms of such maddeningly chaotic configuration that I can only hint at their nature by suggesting the weird paintings that decorate the crypts of the Pharaohs, the carved stele of the mysterious Mayans, the monoliths of Mauna Loa, and the demons of Tibetan sand paintings.

The black priestess — for so I had come to think of her — led our little procession calmly into her realm of chaos and darkness. She was followed by the Gypsy-like Mrs. Llewellyn, then by Lady Fairclough, whose manner appeared as that of a woman entranced.

My own knees, I confess, have begun to stiffen with age, and I was slow to rise to my feet. Holmes followed the procession of women, while I lagged behind. As he was about to enter the opening, Holmes turned suddenly, his eyes blazing. They transmitted to me a message as clear as any words.

This message was reinforced by a single gesture. I had used my hands, pressing against the black floor as I struggled to my feet. They were now at my sides. Fingers as stiff and powerful as a bobby's club jabbed at my waist. The object which Holmes had given me to hold for him was jolted against my flesh, where it created a weird mark which remains visible to this day.

In the moment I knew what I must do.

I wrapped my arms frantically around the black altar, watching with horrified eyes as Holmes and the others slipped from the sealed room into the realm of madness that lay beyond. I stood transfixed, gazing into the Seventh Circle of Dante's hell, into the very heart of Gehenna.

Flames crackled, tentacles writhed, claws rasped, and fangs ripped at suffering flesh. I saw the faces of men and women I had known, monsters and criminals whose deeds surpass my poor talent to record but who are known in the lowest realms of the planet's underworlds, screaming with glee and with agony.

There was a man whose features so resembled those of Lady Fairclough that I knew he must be her brother. Of her missing husband I know not.

Then, looming above them all, I saw a being that must be the supreme monarch of all monsters, a creature so alien as to resemble no organic thing that ever bestrode the earth, yet so familiar that I realized it was the very embodiment of the evil that lurks in the hearts of every living man.

Sherlock Holmes, the noblest human being I have ever encountered, Holmes alone dared to confront this monstrosity. He glowed in a hideous, hellish green flame, as if even great Holmes were possessed of the stains of sin, and they were being seared from within him in the face of this being.

As the monster reached for Holmes with its hideous mockery of limbs, Holmes turned and signaled to me.

I reached within my garment, removed the object that lay against my skin, pulsating with horrid life, drew back my arm, and with a murmured prayer made the strongest and most accurate throw I had made since my days on the cricket pitch of Jammu.

More quickly than it takes to describe, the object flew through the angle. It struck the monster squarely and clung to its body, extending a hideous network of webbing 'round and 'round and 'round.

The monster gave a single convulsive heave, striking Holmes and sending him flying through the air. With presence of mind such as only he, of all men I know, could claim, Holmes reached and grasped Lady Fairclough by one arm and her brother by the other. The force of the monstrous impact sent them back through the angle into the sealed room, where they crashed into me, sending us sprawling across the floor.

With a dreadful sound louder and more unexpected than the most powerful thunderclap, the angle between the walls slammed shut. The sealed room was plunged once again into darkness.

I drew a packet of lucifers from my pocket and lit one. To my surprise, Holmes reached into an inner pocket of his own and drew from it a stick of gelignite with a long fuse. He signaled to me and I handed him another lucifer. He used it to ignite the fuse of the gelignite bomb.

Striking another lucifer, I relit the kerosene lamp that Mrs. Llewellyn had left on the altar. Holmes nodded his approval, and with the great detective in the lead, the four of us — Lady Fairclough, Mr. Philip Llewellyn, Holmes himself, and I — made haste to find our way from the Anthracite Palace.

Even as we stumbled across the great hall toward the chief exit of the palace, there was a terrible rumbling that seemed to come simultaneously from the deepest basement of the building if not from the very center of the earth, and from the dark heavens above. We staggered from the palace — Holmes, Lady Fairclough, Philip Llewellyn, and I — through the howling wind and pelting snow of a renewed storm, through frigid drifts that rose higher than our boot tops, and turned about to see the great black edifice of the Anthracite Palace in flames.

We do hope that you have enjoyed reading this large print book.

Did you know that all of our titles are available for purchase?

We publish a wide range of high quality large print books including:

Romances, Mysteries, Classics
General Fiction
Non Fiction and Westerns

Special interest titles available in large print are:

The Little Oxford Dictionary
Music Book, Song Book
Hymn Book, Service Book

Also available from us courtesy of Oxford University Press:

Young Readers' Dictionary
(large print edition)
Young Readers' Thesaurus
(large print edition)

For further information or a free brochure, please contact us at:
Ulverscroft Large Print Books Ltd.,
The Green, Bradgate Road, Anstey,
Leicester, LE7 7FU, England.
Tel: (00 44) **0116 236 4325**
Fax: (00 44) **0116 234 0205**

Other titles in the
Linford Mystery Library:

RENEGADE LEGIONNAIRE

Gordon Landsborough

General Sturmer, formerly a Nazi officer in the German desert forces, now leads a group of renegade Arab headhunters, tracking down Foreign Legion deserters — a lucrative business. Meanwhile, ex-cowboy Legionnaire Texas is planning revenge. He aims to capture Sturmer and bring him to face justice in America for his war crimes. In Tunisia, during the war, Sturmer had been responsible for the deaths of thousands of prisoners . . . and one of them had been Tex's brother . . .

DEVIL'S PLAGUE

Michael R. Collings

On a summer's morning, a young woman's body lay battered and broken at the bottom of Porcupine Falls. Who was responsible? Was it the local boy, who was so enamoured with her? Or the stranger with the hidden past? And what is the role of the Devil's Plague? It is up to Lynn Hanson and her friend, Victoria Sears, to examine the clues left by the killer and explain the mystery of the death at Porcupine Falls.

CASEY CLUNES INVESTIGATES

Geraldine Ryan

A pregnant Casey Clunes investigates a case of baby snatching. Young Gemma Stebbings' baby has disappeared from the nursery at Brockhaven Hospital. But all the CCTV footage of medical staff and visitors reveals nothing — so where is baby Justin, and who is responsible? *In at the Deep End* finds Casey attending a reception for a Cambridge college's new swimming pool at Doughty Hall. Author Susannah Storey performs the opening ceremony . . . then her dead body is discovered, floating in the pool . . .

THE UNIVERSAL HOLMES

Sherlock Holmes is probably the most popular figure in world literature. For more than a century his adventures have been chronicled in books, on the stage and radio, in motion pictures and television. These Sherlock Holmes adventures show Conan Doyle's detective not only in his earliest days, but also in connection with the works of other authors — Edgar Allan Poe, Edgar Rice Burroughs, H.P. Lovecraft — as Holmes proves himself to be truly *The Universal Holmes*.